# Traveler's Zone

The Revelation Chronicles: Book Two

## Chris Pavesic

Chrispavesic.com

Chris Pavesic
P.O. Box 521
Roscoe, IL 61073
www.chrispavesic.com

Editor: Sloane Taylor

Traveler's Zone/ Chris Pavesic. -- 1st ed.
    ISBN-13: 978-1-949686-02-9

# LOOKING FOR MORE?

Visit chrispavesic.com for more about the author and a complete list of her books.

# PLEASE REVIEW

If you enjoy this novel, please consider leaving a review.

Reviews convince others to give authors like me a chance, so I hope you'll leave one wherever you purchase/review books.

## THANK YOU!

# Cami

### Leggings of Shadow
Defense +20. Type: Medium armor. Item Class: Common. Durability: Unlimited.

### Footpads of Shadow
Type: Medium armor. Item Class: Common. Durability: Unlimited. Attributes: +20 Base Movement Speed. +20 Stealth.

### Bracers of Shadow
Defense +20. Agility: +20 Type: Medium armor. Item Class: Uncommon. Durability: Unlimited.

### Ring of Illumination
Item Class: Common. Durability: Unlimited. Attributes: +20 Spirit.

### Ring of Fierceness
Item Class: Common. Durability: Unlimited. Attributes: +20 Strength.

### Helm of Athene
Stamina: +440. Intellect: +65. Spirit: +90. Type: Medium armor. Item Class: Epic. Durability: 100%. Attributes: Note: Soul-bound upon pickup.

### Harness of Athene
Armor: +465. Agility: +75. Strength: +80. Type: Medium armor. Item Class: Epic. Durability: 100%. Attributes: Note: Soul-bound upon pickup. (2) Set: Reduces the energy costs of all melee abilities and the mana cost of all spells by 5%. (4) Set: Increases the damage dealt by all melee abilities and spells by 10%.

### Bag of Infinite Holding
Item Class: Legendary. Durability: Unlimited. Attributes: Infinite Bag Slots. No weight limit or penalty. Note: Soul-bound. Exclusive to Founders.

### Pointy Stick of Doom
Binds on pickup. Damage: 58-70. Speed: 1.00. Type: Staff. Item Class: Uncommon. Durability: Unlimited: +30 Intellect, +30 Spirit.

# Alby

### Leggings of Shadow
Defense +20. Type: Medium armor. Item Class: Common. Durability: Unlimited.

### Footpads of Shadow
Type: Medium armor. Item Class: Common. Durability: Unlimited. Attributes: +20 Base Movement Speed. +20 Stealth.

### Bracers of Shadow
Defense +20. Agility: +20 Type: Medium armor. Item Class: Uncommon. Durability: Unlimited.

### Ring of Illumination
Item Class: Common. Durability: Unlimited. Attributes: +20 Spirit.

### Ring of Fierceness
Item Class: Common. Durability: Unlimited. Attributes: +20 Strength.

### Cloak of Arachne
Defense: +150. Stamina: +150. Spirit: +25. Intellect: +25. Agility: +25. Strength: =25. Type: Light armor. Item Class: Legendary. Durability: Unlimited. Attributes: Note: Soul-bound upon equip.

### Staff of Infinite Smashing
Binds on pickup. Damage: 65-70. Speed: 1.00. Type: Staff. Item Class: Uncommon. Durability: Unlimited: +30 Intellect, +30 Spirit.

# L.G. Hodag

**Conch Shell Gorget**
Stamina: +75. Armor: =50. Defense: +50. Attack Power: +50. Type: Neckpiece. Item Class: Legendary. Durability: Unlimited. Attributes: Provides protection from all types of poison, disease, magical effects, and venom. Note: Soul-bound upon equip.

**Claws for Alarm**!
Binds on pickup. Damage: 65-70. Speed: 1.00. Type: Fist Weapon Item Class: Uncommon. Durability: Unlimited: +30 Strength, +30 Agility. .

# Prologue

I was born into a world where silicone still ruled. Where the products of the earth outshone those of the sea. Integrated circuits ran all electronic equipment and scientists strove to make the conducting lines smaller and smaller. Silicon Valley tried, and failed, to make chips fast enough to upload human consciousness.

The Revelation came a few years later from the hydrologists. They designed a system that did not use silicone, but instead worked with water molecules. The hydrologists managed to imprint the consciousness of a human mind on a single drop of water.

The water was to be kept in self-contained, sealed aquariums—pure, undiluted, eternal—where virtual realities were constructed to meet every need and desire. All of human knowledge encoded and stored in literal pools of data and integrated with the drops of human consciousness. It was, the hydrologists claimed, utopia achieved.

The obscenely rich were the hydrologist's first clients, many taken near the end of their lives. The procedure did not always work, but there were enough successes to spur people's interest. People suffering from terminal illnesses volunteered to be inscribed, and the hydrologists worked and refined their process. Private companies formed and competition forced price wars. Hundreds of customers grew to thousands, and then to millions. There were landmark court cases arguing whether or not health insurance should cover the cost of the inscription-- whether or not this was a medical procedure designed to save lives or a form of physician assisted suicide. The law struggled to decide if life ended when the body was drained to a dry, leathery husk, or if life continued inside those glowing, sealed aquariums.

I was thirteen when the governments seized control of the laboratories, first in the Eastern European countries. Then the labs of Europe and the Middle East were swallowed up. Terrorist attacks soon followed and destroyed most of the civilized world over the next three years. The United States, Canada, and Greece, those bastions of democracy, did not fall until the very end. Of course, by then no one cared whether or not the government or the private companies ran the uploading programs. Many of the aquariums ruptured in the strife and the droplets, imbued with human consciousness, re-entered the water cycle of the planet.

The destruction of the aquariums led to a moment of serendipity. Once the hydrologists learned that the human minds survived outside of the aquariums, they designed a world-wide system of interlocking realms to host the inscribed human minds. Right now the realms exist in Challenger Deep, the deepest known point in the Earth's seabed hydrosphere, but the hydrologists have plans to expand their reach into the rest of the world. Soon, the only life left on the planet will exist in the virtual world.

Time to play the game.

# Chapter One

The blue light of the construct's life energy illuminates the semi-darkness of the Training Room. A furry creature with burning yellow eyes and a mouthful of sharp teeth turns and hisses at me. I have no time to reflect on what type of creature this might be before the battle is joined. I have the **Spawner** set to random, so I never know what type of foe I will face or how many of the constructs will attack. Will they have claws or weapons? Be melee or ranged? Use magic or steel? Poison or ... the list could go on and on.

You never know what you're going to get when you activate the **Spawner**. All you know is that the creatures are out to kill you. They are set to your level. And to your gear score. With the playing field level, we fight skill-against-skill. I even cancel my Starter Zone immunity to pain upon entering the Training Room to remove that advantage.

I don't want false, easy victories. I want to learn. As my dad used to say, the more you practice, the more you improve your skills, the better chance you have for survival. Just because I'm in a game-like world rather than the real world doesn't make this expression any less true. The game rewards effort and determination. Beating up on creatures less powerful than you teaches nothing.

And I have to be ready. The realms outside the Starter Zone are harsher and more physically and mentally demanding. But I can't stay here if I want to progress in life, if I want to support my family. The safeguards that make the Starter Zone an ideal place to learn about the game also make it limiting.

The gleaming sword in my foe's humanoid hand raises to strike a blow. Being in my fae panther form, I have a few advantages. I make a smaller target for one, and I have claws as well as fangs. On the other side, the construct has a height advantage and can put the weight of its body behind its attacks. I parry and invoke **Claw**, which damages the creature for 10 percent of my Attack Power. The blue light outlining its body starts flickering in response to the damage. I strike it with non-imbued blows, reserving my pool of energy.

The flickering aura indicates the level of my opponent's health and the amount of damage it's taking. Of course, there is a way to work out the mathematics of it all. My trainer, Tanyl, has tried to teach me this over and over to no avail. The visual clues during the fight are better for me than trying to figure out formulas. Along with the flashing aura, I've learned to read the various creatures' body language, the way they move, the speed of the strikes, the telltale positions that indicate weakness or injury.

I'll take this type of knowledge over doing math any day.

The construct manages to strike me with lighting quick movements. I reel under the force of its blows. My armor protects me, but I do take damage. The game's Artificial Intelligence has not chimed in with a warning though, so my health hasn't dipped too far yet.

I have greater maneuverability than this creature and dodge the blows once I get the rhythm of the sword strokes. The creature brings its sword down for a massive hit and I leap sideways. The construct's own momentum carries it forward.

I cast **Claw** again and see the blue light flicker even faster. The creature roars and reels. I cast Maul, which takes more of my energy than **Claw**, but causes damage to a single target for 25 percent of my Attack Power. I slice through the heavily muscled neck. It falls, the blue light extinguishing.

I cast **Slow Heal** on myself, repairing the damage caused during the battle. It erases my physical pain but does not reset the exhaustion I feel. I would need food imbued with special, magical buffs or several hours of sleep to do this. But I can't sleep on most nights, my mind whirling at a million miles a minute. When I do sleep it is interrupted by dreams, by nightmares. So I visit the Training Room to fight until exhaustion overwhelms me. Then I use my **Residence Stone** to magically travel back to the inn I currently call home and sneak into bed without waking my family.

I glance at the clock on the wall above the Spawner controls. Four more hours until dawn. Although it will be a big day, I still have time for one more battle. And then maybe a few hours of uninterrupted sleep thanks to almost total exhaustion.

Our life in the realms is filled with danger, but also with beauty. With hope. Still I have trouble sleeping. I keep revisiting the same scenes in my mind. The scenes that the game made me revisit after I died and before I resurrected, or rezed in game-speak.

#

*"I'm not listing to you!" My voice breaks from the fear and hatred roiling inside of me. "I'm not listening to some ...monster that has taken over my dad's body!"*

*"I'm not leaving," the hydrologist replies. His voice is calm, but his expression is cold. Anyone overhearing our conversation would assume he is the sane one in the room. "I am not leaving until you hear me out and agree to help me."*

*"You'll leave as soon as the water passes through his system," I argue. "This is useless. Why am I arguing with you?"*

*"I don't know you well enough to answer that."*

*"Shut up!"*

*"You can't get rid of me that easy. I'm too experienced at this. I have embedded myself*

*too deep. He'll die of dehydration before eliminating my essence from his system."* He glances at me. *"You are either going to have to help me, or watch your father die."*

#

Why do these scenes keep repeating in my dreams? I don't know. Perhaps it's because I have gotten stronger. I haven't died in game in months and have avoided those nightmare visions. But I do need to sleep. And with sleep comes the nightmares.

I activate the Spawner and move to the middle of the room, waiting to see what type of creature will appear, what type of random construct I will have to face.

It is a good thing I moved. The next humanoid creature that appears, bellowing a war-cry, is huge and has altogether too many limbs. It towers above me, a war hammer, broad axe, and long sword clutched in its three hands. It sees me and swings the broad axe.

I leap out of the way, rolling forward and through its legs to position for a rear attack. I invoke **Claw** and follow up immediately with **Bite**, which damages the target for 20 percent of my Attack Power.

The blue light of the construct barely flickers. I haven't done much damage. The creature's third arm, which is placed slightly behind the other two on its body and holds the war hammer, crashes down.

A good blow. I see actual stars behind my eyes as I stumble backward, tasting coppery blood in my mouth.

*Warning: Your health has dipped below 80%.*

The AI has chimed in at last. I dodge a cut from the longsword and retreat, casting **Slow Heal**, trying to keep a safe distance from my opponent until I can realign my senses.

The construct doesn't allow me time to recuperate. It rushes me, swinging the war hammer, which I dodge. I counter-attack with a fury, casting **Claw**, **Bite**, and **Maul** in a sequence designed to do maximize damage while not draining my energy too quickly. The aura of blue light begins flickering faster.

The creature roars and kicks, punting me like a furry football. I crash against the far wall, losing my breath as the air is knocked out of my lungs. Explosions of burning pain rack my body, but I use the momentum of my collision and continue to roll because my opponent is rushing headlong at me, bellowing in anger.

*Warning: Your health has dipped below 60%.*

My breath comes in labored gasps, but I regain my feet before the construct reaches me. It swipes the broad axe at me and I duck. The axe head slams into the wall.

A look of puzzlement fills the creature's face as it tugs on the weapon, trying to pull it free. I use this moment of distraction to attack again, running through my regular attack sequence. The blue aura flashes faster as the construct's body takes more and more damage.

With a rapid movement my adversary abandons the axe and grabs me around the neck, slamming my body against the wall. Explosions of burning pain make it difficult to focus. I dig my claws into the construct's arms, trying to force them from my throat.

*Warning: Your health has dipped below 50%.*

*Warning: Your health has dipped below 40%.*

*Warning: Your health has dipped below 30%.*

The AI warnings are coming fast and furious now, but I will not give up. Using my back legs, I tear at its chest, raking and kicking with all of my might. I can't magically imbue attacks from my feet, but they do damage.

Its grip slackens, and I drop to the floor. The construct tumbles forward, slumping against the wall, its eyes close. With a last flash of blue light, it disappears. Nothing remains to show it ever existed. Even the imbedded axe dissolves without leaving damage to the wall.

Lying prone on the Training Room floor, I have just enough mana left to cast **Slow Heal** one last time. I wait until it mends the worst of my wounds and then use my **Residence Stone**. It glows brighter and brighter until my surroundings disappear. Ten seconds later I arrive at the inn, ready to crawl into bed and slip into slumber.

Perhaps tonight I won't dream.

# Chapter Two

The gaslights sputter, dim, and then extinguish. My little sister, Alby, reaches out to take my hand. I give her fingers a reassuring squeeze.

"Cami?" she asks. "What's going on?"

"A surprise," I say. I make my tone as reassuring as possible. After all we have been through in the last few years I don't want her to worry. I want her to enjoy this.

The door to the kitchen swings open and a waitress appears, her face illuminated by the glow of candles on top of a layer cake. Eight candles for eight years.

"Happy birthday!" I exclaim. The waitress, a non-player character, or NPC, named Nellie, places the cake directly in front of my sister. It is a work-of-art, decorated with enough frosting shaped into vines, leaves, and flowers to fill a cottage garden.

"Here you go ladies."

"Grrarrg?" L.G., our hodag companion, growls playfully.

"Ladies and gentleman," Nellie corrects herself.

"Wow!" Alby grins at us. "The frosting-flowers are pretty. And so many colors. Is it chocolate cake?"

"Of course," Nellie replies, as if any other kind would be unthinkable. "With vanilla frosting."

"Frosting," L.G. says in his gravelly voice. He smiles and his fangs glow in the candlelight. "Hodags like vanilla frosting."

"Frosting is the best part of the cake," I agree. I reach over and rub the fur behind L.G.'s horns. It's his favorite place to be scratched. He twitches his tail in appreciation.

"Time to sing." Nellie joins in our rather out-of-tune rendition of the birthday song. Alby applauds our efforts and then leans forward to blow out the candles.

"Remember to make a wish," I urge.

"Wish," L.G. echoes.

Nellie turns the gaslights back on. It's early in the morning and the restaurant is empty except for the four of us. The sun hasn't even popped over the horizon. "Are you sure that's all you want to eat? I can whip up some eggs and bacon right quick. And a chef's salad for Mr. L.G."

"No thank you." One of the best parts of living in the realms is the food, and we do have a fondness for Nellie's cooking. Most days we have at least one meal here.

But it really doesn't matter what we eat if we are not looking for specific magical buffs, like increased health or stamina. As players we can get nutrition from any type of food. We don't have to worry about eating a balanced diet. Or gaining weight for that matter.

So eating birthday cake for breakfast is entirely appropriate. Heck, eating birthday cake for every meal over the next ten years would be okay. But I wouldn't want to limit myself. One of the hydrologists must have been a gourmet chef in the real world because every dish we've tried here tastes fantastic. It's like an explosion of flavor whenever I put food into my mouth.

Last year at this time, Alby and I were living in the real world, hiding from the looter gangs, and terrified of losing our minds to inscribed water. We had found temporary shelter in the basement of a burned-out house. I managed to scavenge a can of tuna that we shared for our only meal of the day. I sang the birthday song then, too, in a low whisper so I wouldn't alert anyone to our presence, but didn't discuss making a wish. We went to sleep hungry, thirsty, and afraid.

What a difference a year makes.

Little by little that fear and desperation are fading into memory, just something that had happened instead of a time so vivid it brings cold sweat out onto my skin every time I visit those memories. I doubt they will fade altogether. Although it does feel like I am working the poison of those thoughts out of my system as I adjust to our new life.

In the realms Alby has flourished, and it shows more on her frame than mine. As the first of our family to be inscribed, the hydrologists designated me our family's Founder. I was able to take an adult player form even though I was only sixteen. My appearance is locked in place unless I pay an in-game fee at a beauty shop to have it altered.

Since Alby entered the Realms as a juvenile, her in-game body can change and adapt as she matures. She has grown at least two inches since we were inscribed. I'm curious to see if she will be taller than me when she becomes an adult.

Being shorter than my little sister would be weird.

When they are first inscribed, Players have the choice of being dwarves, humans, shifters, or fae. Family members tend to choose the same race, but it's not a requirement. Alby and I both chose fae for our characters after meeting Darlene, a fae hydrologist, in the realm sorting area.

With the choice of a human or a dwarf, Darlene had explained, you would start to get into sub-categories. Players will either be magic workers—mages or wizards—or specialize in martial training—warriors or thieves. A warrior will never be able to work a magic spell while a wizard cannot develop enough strength to wield a sword effectively. They are locked into their class roles.

Shifters also have limitations. Both the vampires and werewolves are magic workers, but that magic is tied into their non-human aspect. They are ineffective during the daylight.

The fae are the most complex characters in the realms. They work spells like both mages and wizards—damage and healing—and can fight like warriors and thieves. They can shift to a panther form but are not limited to the night.

There are drawbacks, of course. Because of the way the game distributes attributes like strength, intellect, agility, and spirit, fae are hard to level once a player leaves the Starter Zone. Fae have to learn all of the branches of combat, not just one. And since the others can specialize, most people assume a fae is at a disadvantage having only half the attributes of the other classes.

Darlene explained that this equal distribution is actually an advantage if you think about it correctly. During a fight a fae can shift forms, attack both with magic and martial skills, and cast heals on him or herself. We may not be the best at any one type of combat, but we have multiple skill sets up our sleeves. If we study and learn how to use them, we can win any fight.

But what really sold both Alby and me is the ability only the fae and vampires have in the realms. Upon reaching level twenty, fae learn **Flightform**. Others can use mounts, airships, or magic carpets. But fae can shift into a black falcon and instantly take wing.

How cool is that?

Alby cuts the cake. Nellie looks surprised when Alby offers her a piece.

"Oh, hunny, I'm not supposed to eat with the customers."

"We're the only ones here. We won't tell if you don't." I wink at her. My stomach rumbles. I can smell the chocolate mixed with the strong scent of vanilla and cream.

"Well, maybe just a bite. That frosting does look good."

"Good," L.G. agrees, licking his lips. He attacks the cake with gusto. A daub of frosting lands on his nose.

"Slow down there, little guy, or you'll get the hiccups." I use my napkin to clean his face. He grins at me.

L.G. has grown too. When we first met him in the Spider Queen's cavern, he was small enough to ride on our shoulders, perched like a parrot. Now he is the same size as a golden retriever. If he keeps up this growth rate, by next year he won't need to sit on a chair to eat at the table.

Looking at my small family causes tears of happiness to threaten. I'm so proud of Alby, of how fast she has adjusted to life in the realms. And I couldn't imagine life without L.G. Every day he does something to make me smile.

We are safe here in the Starter Zone. It is familiar and comfortable. It's secure.

Which makes it even harder to know that we have to leave today.

# Chapter Three

"The party isn't over just yet. L.G. and I have something for you." I pull out a small, colorfully wrapped box topped with a red bow.

"Did you wrap that?" Alby asks.

"No. The shopkeeper did," I admit.

"Thought so."

"Hey! Just because I got tangled up in tape that one time." I grin. "I'm surprised you remember. You were pretty young."

"There are some things you just don't forget." She says this in a smug voice, but the corner of her mouth quirks upward.

My sister. She's ninety-nine percent angel. But, oh ... that one percent. Trust her to remember the fiasco when I tried to use packing tape for gift wrapping.

This happened on the Christmas Eve before the world went to heck-in-a-handbasket, when we were still safe in our house. In our subdivision. In our town. When we could go to the mall and buy all types of useless, pretty trinkets. With my allowance I purchased Alby a sand-art kit and wanted to wrap it myself. I couldn't find the scotch tape, so I decided to use packing tape.

At first I pulled pieces of tape that were too long. They stuck together. I had quite a pile of clumped tape on the floor. Then the dispenser jammed. I stood on it and pulled the tape upward with all of my strength. When it came loose I lost my balance and fell into the mess. I wasn't hurt, but dad needed an hour to unstick the clumped tape from my hair. Afterward he wrapped the gift while I "supervised."

Alby loved the sand-art kit. She made a different picture every day for a week. Her small fingers were adept at lifting the edges of the sticky paper to peel it back. She sprinkled just the right amount of colored sand to fill in each area.

After she completed the pictures, Dad hung them on the fridge, using magnets to keep them in place. We ate our meals looking at my sister's masterpieces. I hated to leave them behind when we fled the house after dad died.

The memory twists my insides into a knot. But the pictures weren't necessary for survival. Back then we traveled light. We only carried what we needed to survive.

And at that point they had been spattered with my dad's blood.

I clear my mind, focusing on the here and now. I don't want to think about the past. I don't want to dwell on the darkness and the sadness of the world before we entered the realms, but sometimes it creeps through the walls I placed around my memories.

I don't want to ruin my sister's special day.

"Can I open it now?"

"Yep."

Alby tugs on the bow and the wrappings disappear with a poof. No matter what anyone might think about the hydrologists, they certainly love dramatic effects. They also must dislike trash, because the bow disappears right out of her hand.

A satchel appears on the table. Made out of rich brown leather, it looks just like a college-kid's book bag. It is actually too large to have fit in the box.

Ah well, it's magic. The laws of physics sort of fly out the window in the realms. I've grown to expect these types of miracles. And even to enjoy them.

And speaking of magic, the AI interface chimes in with its old-fashioned computer-generated voice the minute the satchel appears.

*Your group member has received:*
**Materials Bag.**
   *Item Class: Epic.*
   *Durability: Unlimited.*
   *Attributes: Infinite Bag Slots.*
   *No weight limit or penalty.*
   *Limitations: Holds only materials.*
   *Note: Soul-bound when equipped.*

The AI is keeping me updated, but I already knew all of this. I heard it when I bought the gift. Where I once thought the old-fashioned computer voice was helpful, I have revised my opinion. But the irritation is a small price to pay to live in the Realms.

"Cami!" Alby's eyes sparkle. "It's wonderful! But ... can we afford it?"

The satchel is expensive, costing 500 gold coins. And our funds are limited. But I don't want her to worry.

"You need it, so we can afford it." I wink at L.G. "I can't keep carrying all of the stuff you collect, you little pack rat."

"Pack rat," he agrees.

When we first joined the Realms I entered as a Founder and received certain perks. One item, a **Bag of Infinite Holding**, has been extremely useful. Like Alby's new bag, it has infinite slots and no weight limit or penalty. However, my bag can hold any type of item.

As a regular player, Alby's original bag has 25 slots. Each item she picks up adds to the weight until it's too heavy to carry. So when her bag is full, she passes me the items. I carry them until we return to town and stop by the bank to deposit her treasures.

**Bags of Infinite Holding** are unique to Founders. Since I can't get her that, I bought the next-best type of bag for a Player. A **Materials Bag** has infinite slots, but only for gathered items like flowers, herbs, berries, vegetables, ore, chopped wood, and so forth. And when placed in the bag, those items won't weigh her down.

She'll have to store items like gear, weapons, or the leftover pieces of birthday cake in her other bag. But this should give her enough extra room for a while.

"It's beautiful," Nellie says. "The color matches your eyes."

Alby's eyes are the only part of her that isn't a shade of green.

"Thanks ..." Alby starts, but is interrupted by a harsh voice.

"What is wrong with you!"

"There's nothing wrong with me! It's all them."

Although the speakers are outside the restaurant, their voices override ours.

"Those two are at it early," Nellie comments during a break in the action.

I shake my head. "I wonder what it is this time?" The two Players, Kickerz and Wink Girl, have been arguing more frequently in recent weeks. They don't appear to care that their conflict is public. And really, it's hard to figure out why they are arguing. Most of the time it doesn't make much sense.

"Really?" Wink Girl asks.

"Yes really! The guild leader is a b****." The automatic curse blocker filters obscures Kickerz language, but the meaning is clear.

"How is your missing a raid date the guild leader's fault?"

"She said the raid was scheduled for Tuesday. That could be any dang Tuesday of the week!"

Silence.

"Well? No clever comment?" he asks. "That's hard to believe. Your mouth's been running all day."

"It takes me a minute to process this level of stupidity all at once."

# Chapter Four

"**H**ow dare you call me stupid!"

"I didn't know it would hurt your feelings. I thought you already knew."

"Whatever." His voice drips with disgust. "I'm done."

"I'd like to leave you with a thought, but I'm not sure you have anywhere to put it."

Wink Girl enters into the restaurant alone and sits near the door. She's a beautiful human player with long, blond hair pulled into a loose braid and fair, clear skin. Normally she has bright eyes and a lively smile. But her eyes look swollen, like she has been crying. And her lips are pressed into a thin line.

"I'll bring you a menu and some ice water," Nellie calls to her. She jumps to her feet but takes a moment to smile at my sister. "Breakfast is on me, ladies and gent. No ifs, ands, or buts. You only turn eight once."

"Thank you," we chorus.

"Any fun plans for the day?"

"We're going to get our Homestead," Alby pipes up.

"We have to go to MidWorld to pick it out," I add.

"You're moving on? Does that mean I won't be seeing you again?"

"We'll still be coming in occasionally. I can't cook as well as you." I smile and turn toward my sister. "And don't think I can't see you and L.G. smirking about that."

"You're cooking is good, Cami, especially if you like lumpy bread."

"And burnt bits," L.G. adds.

"Don't dis the burnt bits. That's fiber," I say.

We gather the leftovers and head toward the door. Passing by Wink Girl's table, I'm not sure what to do. She is one of the few players in the Realms that we talk to with any degree of friendliness.

But we're not friends. Not exactly. I don't know if I will ever trust another human being enough to call him or her my friend. I distance myself from people for many reasons. Experience in the real world has drilled the fact into my head that my fellow human beings don't keep their words.

I can't trust people when all I have from the past is evidence why I shouldn't.

"Are you okay, Miss Wink?" Alby asks, making the decision for me.

Wink Girl snaps her gaze in our direction, like she is seeing us for the first time.

"Oh, hi girls. And L.G." She tries to smile.

"Would you like a piece of birthday cake?" Alby offers her a slice.

"Thank you." Her voice trembles and she clears her throat. "You can't be sad when eating birthday cake, my mom used to say."

"Why are you sad?" I ask. I can't help myself. Her eyes fill with unshed tears.

"It's Kickerz. He's ... being an idiot again. Got us thrown out of the guild."

"Isn't that the second one this week?" I ask, and then inwardly flinch. Sometimes my mouth runs ahead of my brain. I don't want to make her feel worse.

When we first met them, Kickerz and Wink Girl had been in Ahahahahaha, a guild that accepts younger members who are confined to the Starter Zone. Over the last few months they had cycled through Omnium Domini,

Hard to Ignore, Unwavering, and Urban Achievers.

I don't know much about guilds, other than the fact that a lot of people join them. They recruit members daily in the Old Town square. And they declare war on each other, the older members fighting beyond the borders of the Starter Zone in PVP areas, the younger ones engaging in one-on-one duels to "support their side."

Even though players can't die in the realms, it seems like a terrible waste of time and effort. In my mind I picture the looter gangs we avoided in the real world. Their wars took place in the streets where people didn't magically resurrect when they died. They left the bodies as macabre trophies to mark their territories.

I don't want any part of this for myself or for Alby and L.G.

"Yeah, and we will both be eighteen in the next few weeks. He'll want to start exploring the realms and we won't have anyone to back us up."

"You'll have each other," I say.

"You'd think so, wouldn't you." She picks at the cake with a fork. "He's off trying to join TOP MEN."

"Isn't that the guild that accepts only male players?"

"After all we've been through, my boyfriend apparently doesn't see anything wrong with excluding me." A tear drops off her chin and lands on the tablecloth. "Things are getting worse faster than I can lower my standards. I'm at the point in my life when I need a stronger word than f***."

I have a feeling we'd be blushing if it wasn't for the curse-blocker.

"Maybe he'll change his mind," Alby says.

"Maybe." She sighs. "Don't ever fall in love. Take my advice. It isn't worth the heartache. You expect more from someone because you love them, and don't realize that they're unbelievably stupid."

We leave the restaurant and head out of the center of the town to a glade that has been formed by dark, sweet-smelling ornament trees. They curve in a semicircle around a much larger tree in the center. Its canopy spreads out almost to the edge of the glade. We walk underneath the branches and move closer to the trunk and to the round wooden door in its center.

Before we can knock, the door opens, revealing a grumpy looking fae dressed in a pine-green tunic and a white pair of breeches. His hair and beard are as silver as my own, but his skin is nut brown and smooth. Even though I am seven feet tall and almost match him in height, he manages to look down his nose at me.

*Fae Trainer: Tanyl Xillamin*
*Level: 20*
*Alignment: Friendly*

I sigh. We have spent almost every day for the last few months training with Tanyl, honing our skills. I know his name. I know his profession, his level, and our alignment because I hear it from the AI every day.

Every freaking day.

"You're late," Tanyl says in way of greeting.

"I didn't know we were on a schedule," I reply.

"Players! Think the world revolves around them," he mutters, urging us into his home. "Up the stairs, please, third level."

The outer walls of the tree are lined with bookshelves filled with tomes and volumes of all sorts and sizes. During breaks from our training sessions, Tanyl would feed us cookies and urge us to read. Thus we were familiar with a lot of the books on the lower level, but as we climb I realize how many books his library actually holds.

This is something we can have in our Homestead. I feel a surge of pleasure. A library of our own.

Making the decision to get the Homestead has taken me months. I wanted to wait until Alby reached level 20 and could fly using the **Flightform** spell. That way she could get around on her own while L.G. used the **Flying Carpet**, a special quest reward I received from Tanyl. Then I wanted to wait until we had completed all of the quests in the Starter Zone. And then ... I ran out of excuses. Ones that I could share with Alby and L.G. at least.

The Starter Zone is safe. We had the choice to remain here, back when we first started training with Tanyl. But I didn't take it. I couldn't.

No matter how comfortable we would be, without the ability to move forward, without new challenges and new experiences, it would be a prison.

Safety is one thing. Stagnation is another.

And I'm interested in exploring this world. Seeing what it has to offer.

Alby can't come with me yet into the regular realms. You need to be eighteen years old to leave the Starter Zone or other safe areas like the Homesteads. I'm seventeen, but I qualify because I am also our family's Founder. That status gives me a lot of perks.

But Alby can go to one of the schools while I explore. She's been buzzing with excitement about becoming a tinkerer. And a potion maker. And an armorer. And a weapon smith. And so many other things. But before she can do that, we need to set up our Homestead.

Tanyl hustles us into a room that is filled with pods that look like they were pulled from some sort of futuristic space ship. The top and the bottom of each pod is a flat disc that has been carved out of marble and etched with symbols. Each has a distinct pattern. A beam of blue, sparkly light fills the exact center of one pod. The others have red beams in the same position.

*Warning! You are approaching a one-way Transport Portal. Review: Yes/No?*

"Yes."

*Transport Portals allow travel between distant points in the realm. A player or NPC can step into the light and be instantly transported to MidWorld or one of the major cities in the realms. Each transport portal is linked to a specific other portal and can only be changed by its owner or a designated user.*

*Transport portals are programmed as one-way or two-way. One-way portals allow travel from Point A to Point B, but do not allow return travel along the same path. Two-way transport portals allow free travel between Point A and Point B. They are extremely rare.*

*Learn more about programming a Transport Portal? Yes/No?*

"No." There will be plenty of time to learn about that in the future. And I'm sure I will hear about it from the AI. Over and over again.

"Is it safe?" Alby asks.

"Yes," Tanyl replies. "This portal leads to MidWorld. The other portals lead to the major cities in Realm One, Two, and Three. But you can't use them yet. They're locked until you physically visit the cities. It's a precaution so that players cannot transport to areas too high for their levels."

"So we walk into the blue light and end up at MidWorld?"

This earns me an arched eyebrow. "Very succinctly stated."

"Cool."

"And now you're back to normal."

I grin.

"The first time you use a portal it is best to do it as fast as possible. Don't linger in the light. Step forward. And for heaven's sake, don't jump." He shakes his head. "Every player thinks it's a new idea to jump through the portal. That it's somehow," he narrows his eyes at me, "cool."

"Gotcha," I say, winking at Alby and L.G. "Meet you two on the other side."

I walk up to the blue light and jump.

# Chapter Five

When I enter the Transport Portal the light surrounds me. The indefinable fission of stepping through an event horizon and launching forward through a bolt of blue light. My body dissolves like sugar melting in water. Cold, then warm, then icy.

The disorientation of travel makes my head throb and throws off my balance. The jump makes it worse. I manage to keep on my feet as I emerge from the portal, but I'm close to face-planting on marble floor.

Alby and L.G. follow mere seconds behind. They didn't jump, so are in slightly better shape.

"He told you about the jumping to work on you," Alby says. She's grinning. "He knew you couldn't resist."

"It was a trap and I walked right into it," I agree.

"You okay?" L.G. asks in his gravely voice.

"Yep. Just need to catch my breath." I smile to reassure them, although my stomach has a major butterfly convention going on inside. "No more jumping through portals for me."

The area where we emerged from the teleport is empty. I walk through it, waving my hand, but do not encounter any resistance. There is no return portal in this area. So the trip really is one-way.

The room is sparsely decorated, but I recognize the general setting from the day we joined the Realms. There are screen banks on the walls. Pastel-colored blobs move in random patterns on the screens, creating a soothing effect. But I wonder if someone is monitoring them and observing us. We have to be very careful with what we say when we are in MidWorld. I had cautioned both Alby and L.G. to let me do most of the talking before we left our room at the inn. They are both young enough that they agreed without argument. Neither one of them knows the truth behind our entry into the Realms, and I intend to keep it that way.

"Hello girls. Right on time." Darlene, the fae Hydrologist who helped us choose our realm and Player forms, walks through a blank area of the wall with a flash of blue light. "Oh, and a little, green fellow."

"Hi Darlene. This is L.G. Hodag. He's part of our family," Alby says. L.G. grins at Darlene. His fangs flash white.

"I see. Okay." She checks the information on her tablet. "No problem. He's been officially registered."

"It's nice to see you again," I say. Talking to Hydrologists is dangerous, which is another reason I avoided choosing the Homestead for as long as possible. I try to be polite without saying much. I don't want them looking into our situation too closely. At any moment they might figure out that we're frauds. That we didn't pay to be in the realms. And that would be a disaster.

There are only two types of humans in the realms. Players and slaves.

Most of the beings Players interact with are artificially generated NPCs with varying degrees of intellect and autonomy. But there are some NPCs that are enslaved humans, inscribed against their will and forced to serve. This is more than a lifetime sentence, since humans cannot truly die in the realms. We can be injured and killed, but unlike the game-generated NPCS, we are resurrected. So an enslaved human will be trapped in his or her NPC role forever with no way to escape.

It's a fate worse than death.

"Come on. I'll show you the models. There are three basic ones to choose from, and then you can pick the add-ons." She heads toward the door and we follow.

"Add-ons?" I ask.

"Oh yes. The designers have spent years putting together models for homes. There's buildings and furniture. We have patterns for almost anything you can imagine. That's our motto: 'If you can imagine it, you can live it!' If you want something special, you can contract for that. All it takes is money." Darlene laughs. "Not much different than our prior lives, is it?"

The monetary system in the realms is set up in a fairly easy manner with the categories of coins moving from copper to bronze, then silver to gold, and finally to platinum. One hundred copper coins are worth one bronze coin, and so forth up the line.

Because of the mix-up during our inscription, I scammed a single platinum coin from the Hydrologists. I invested that in the

Realms bank where it earns a steady one percent interest. It has generated 5 thousand gold coins during our time in the Realms.

That's our cushion in case we need it for an emergency. Does this qualify? I don't know. I will wait to learn what Darlene has to say before I decide.

We earned money doing the Starter Zone quests, but not much, and spent most of it on housing and food. Low-level quests pay a few copper coins at the start and work their way up to bronze. The gear and other item drops aren't worth much either after vendoring. The only other money in my possession I looted from a chest in the Spider Queen's lair. It was substantial. 25 thousand gold coins. But that was a one-in-a-million rare event and not something I will ever be able to duplicate again. And I had spent some of the gold on Alby's gift.

So money is in short supply. Although we do have more wealth in the Realms than we ever did in the real world, we're not rich. We don't have the type of income that the other players brought with them when they purchased their spots.

And the schools Alby wants to attend will cost money. The classes themselves are free for players with Homesteads, but students need specific materials in order to learn their professions. From what I have been able to learn those costs can add up.

Darlene leads us to a richly furnished room with plush carpets and three leather-bound chairs. The chairs are big enough to accommodate our fae form, which is much larger than a human. L.G. joins Alby on her chair and curls up head to tail.

"Ohh, it feels nice to get off my feet for a while," Darlene says. "It's been an exhausting night. We're getting ready to launch Phase Two and everyone is pulling extra shifts."

"Did you get your Homestead yet?" I ask. "You wanted to set up a ranch where you could keep horses, right?"

Darlene waves her hand at a blank wall and pulls up a map, the image zooming in on the area I recognize as Realm One. "Not yet. I'm still saving my money. I hope that I can afford one while there are spaces left near the inner rim."

"Inner rim?" Alby asks.

"MidWorld is the safest place in the Realms. The center of the world so to speak. And if you remember in Phase One we set up three Realms. You chose to live in Realm One, my favorite," she said with a smile. "High Fantasy mixed with a touch of steampunk. But the others are good too. Urban Fantasy in Realm Two and an Old West vibe in Realm Three. So exiting. You can visit each one, you know, now that you are getting your Homestead. Each one has its own Starter Zone area, so underaged players have new territory to explore too."

"I remember." All the Realms have a mixture of magic and technology. Now that we know more about our own Realm, the concepts of the other two are easier to understand. They might be fun to explore at some point in the future. The problem, though, is time. We have so much to learn about Realm One that exploring the others is not a priority.

"And those first three Realms will always be the safest. Less chance for drifting."

"What does that mean?" Alby asks. "The AI doesn't say when I ask."

Darlene waves her hand at the screen and pulls up a picture of a circle. The small, inner part of the circle is dark red. The outer part of the circle is divided into three equal sections of blue, green, and black.

"This might make it clearer. It's a pie chart representation of our world. The red dot in the center is MidWorld and the other three are the Realms."

"Sort of looks like a dart board." I frown. "But the world isn't really flat. In the Realms, I mean."

"No." She shakes her head. "This is over-simplified to help you grasp the concepts."

"Okay. Simple is good." As long as I don't have to do math, I'm happy.

Darlene gestures at the screen and the picture zooms in on the red circle. "This is what we call the inner rim. The portion of our world immediately surrounding MidWorld."

"Okay," Alby, L.G., and I say.

She waves her hand once again and the picture resumes its original form. "The current outer rim encircles Realms One, Two, and Three. In Phase Two, we will be adding more Realms, sort of another circle around the outside, and then the first three realms will be designated the Inner Realms."

"You're just going to keep adding to the circle until you enclose the whole earth?" I think about the people still living in the real world. Still surviving. Even though we've been inscribed for only six months, our lives outside of the realms feels like a fading nightmare. Scrounging for food. Terrified of untreated water. Hiding from the looter gangs. Hungry. Thirsty. Always afraid.

"Exactly!" She waves her hand and the familiar Realm One picture appears. "But until we finish all phases of the project, the safest part of the Realms will be those closest to MidWorld. There is less chance of uninscribed water drifting into the Realms and disrupting the patterns."

"What happens if you get caught by the drifting water?" I ask.

"It's fairly dangerous. You can get pulled out of the Realms and caught up in the water cycle of the planet."

I shudder at the thought and slide my arms around my shoulders. Stuck in the endless water cycle, helpless to direct your actions. Month after month, year after year, passing through plants, consumed by animals. How much of your mind is left after that? No wonder that people generally act crazy after drinking inscribed water. The inscribed minds that enter their bodies can't be sane.

"But that's nothing for you girls to worry about." Darlene's voice pulls me back from my musings. "You two are getting one of the safest homesteads available."

L.G. raises his head, frowning at the omission, but Darlene doesn't even notice. She's concentrating on the screen. Pulling up another series of pictures.

Since we are grouped I can pick up the emotions of the others. L.G.'s confusion and Alby's growing irritation at Darlene's attitude. They'll be less inclined to say anything to her, which is better for all of us.

It's an attitude I've noticed before. Hydrologists and the other players don't think of NPCs as people. They tend to treat NPCs as disposable. Inconsequential.

But Alby and I have friends in the Realms. Beings we do trust because of their actions and natures. All of them are NPCs.

And L.G. is special. He's family.

The more I think about it, the more I wonder about the disparity between Players and NPCs. We're all just minds and bodies made of inscribed water. The only real difference? Money and power.

Even if I wasn't worried about exposing our secrets, I wouldn't feel comfortable talking openly to Darlene. She acts friendly, but it's her job. We're paying customers, so she puts on a fake smile and offers to solve our problems. And any seed of trust planted by that insincere friendliness will bear bitter fruit.

# Chapter Six

"This is so exciting!" Darlene smiles. "There are three basic biomes for the homestead in Realm One. The first is the Grassy Woodlands model. The ground is level for the most part. There are a few hills, many varieties of trees, and a large lake. Based on variations built into the model, there are a random number of ponds and rivers."

The screen reveals an unexpectedly beautiful scene. A small wooded area beside a large lake, the woods following and hugging the banks, leading to cleared land, gently rolling and lushly green, dotted with wildflowers.

"So pretty." Alby's face lights up looking at the flowers.

"The second biome is the Winter Wonderland model," Darlene shifts the screen to an image of snow-covered rolling hills, blue skies, and towering mountain peaks with snowflakes falling though the air. "This is popular among players who enjoy skiing and other winter sports. If you choose this model, we have several chalet and lodge house patterns. There are even steam-powered ski lifts you can purchase."

"Why steam-powered?" I ask.

"Rules of the Realms." She smiles at me. "The only technology in Realm One is steam-powered."

"I remember you talking about that when we made our realm choice. Steampunk, right?" I hesitate. "I haven't seen much of that."

"The amount of technology is limited in the Starter Zone. It's set up so that you first learn about magic and your own abilities and talents. But just wait until you take your first trip on a luxury steampunk airship. You won't want to travel any other way."

The snowscape beautiful, but cold and uninviting. I can't imagine living there with no chance to have a garden. And I've never skied in my life.

"The third biome is the Seaside Vacation model. Warm, sunny days, white sand beaches, tropical trees. It's our most popular model. And we have a great many patterns for seaside cottages and estates."

The beach and blue ocean are very pretty, but it's not for us. We want a place where we can grow our own food and be self-sufficient. The only thing that seems to be growing in this biome are palm trees and some silvery-green grass.

"We would like the first one. The Grassy Woodland," I say.

"Wonderful! You'll be very happy there I'm sure!" Darlene flashes us a professional smile and makes a notation on her tablet.

I'm sure she would say the same thing no matter which one we chose.

"Lot's of green leafies," L.G. says.

"Exactly." I reach over to scratch behind his horns.

Darlene frowns. "Ah, yes. That leads me to the matter of the NPC."

"His name's L.G." Alby says. She puts her arm around him.

"Of course, dear." Darlene plasters the smile back on her face. "I just want to give your sister some options."

"Options?" I feel a chill slip over my skin.

"Each homestead comes with one incorporated NPC. It's built into the price you paid when you purchased your entry into the Realms. This NPC has the same abilities and sentience of a player. Including the ability to resurrect. Usually that NPC is your main servant and runs a homestead. Like a butler or maid. Someone to organize everything. Make purchases and keep the household running. And provide information. Your own personal NPClopedia." She laughs.

Darlene had made the same joke the first time we met. I find it even less funny now. "What are you saying exactly?"

"You have a few choices. You can go without a main human servant, of course, but I don't recommend that. You can pay for another NPC. The current price is 50 thousand gold. Or you can replace the hodag NPC with one of the official models."

"No!" Alby jumps to her feet and stands between Darlene and L.G. Her face flushes a dark green, her hands clench in fists at her sides. "No, you can't have him!"

I'm on my feet as well. With one sweep of my arm, I push her behind me, blocking both my sister and L.G. from Darlene's sight.

"Not an option," I say harshly, because I'm as upset as Alby. "L.G. is a member of our family."

Darlene has drawn back as far as she can into the chair. Her cheeks flare with color. "Please, I didn't mean to upset you." Her voice has a let's-be-reasonable tone that sets my teeth on edge.

"No more talk about getting rid of L.G." I say.

She nods and we resume our seats. Alby wraps her arms around L.G.s neck and they both glare at Darlene. My little sister is wary. And she doesn't forgive easily. She'll never trust Darlene now. Neither will L.G.

But I have to be smarter. I don't want to make an enemy of Darlene, or any of the Hydrologists. They built this world. In a larger sense they control it. Sure there are rules to protect Players, but our position is more tenuous than Alby and L.G. realize. I have to protect them from dangers they don't know even exist.

"You couldn't know how much he means to us," I say with a consolatory smile.

The false smile returns to Darlene's face. It is calculated to make us forget that she had intended to kill L.G. just moments earlier. But the smile stops well short of her eyes. They are still cool and sharp. "Of course. I was just trying to save you a bit of money." She clasps her hands together. "But if you want to purchase another NPC, far be it from me to—"

"I don't want to live with a stranger," Alby interrupts her. She's still glaring.

"We'll skip that for now." I decide. "What else do we need for the Homestead?"

"Each Homestead comes with a starter package, which includes 5 pre-programed one-way portals, 1 building pattern, 1 fabricator, 1 forge, and 1 gauntlet."

Okay. I understand the portals and will learn more about them through use. And we have used fabricators and forges during some of our quests in the Starter Zone. Forges let players turn items like ore into bars, and the fabricators turn the bars into different components for crafting. There are ones available to use in the Starter Zone, but having these devices in our Homestead will be convenient.

"What does a gauntlet do?"

"It helps you place items in your Homestead when you are building. Or clearing items away."

"Clearing items?"

"Yes. If you want to level the ground to build a cottage, for example, you can use the gauntlet to pick up the dirt, grass, and rocks. You can also use it to place items like large blocks of stone. Items that would be too heavy for you to lift on your own."

I frown. "We've seen people building in the realms, but they don't seem to be using gauntlets. We even helped raise a barn for one quest."

"Gauntlets don't work in the realms. Only in the Homesteads. Because changes in the realms are not permanent. They cycle."

"Like the barn we built. A month later it burned down. We joined the quest to help fight the fire."

"Right. And a few weeks later Players would have the opportunity to help build that barn again."

"That kind of stinks for the NPCs who live on the farm."

"They don't know any better." Darlene dismisses the thought with a wave of her hand.

But they do. At least in the Starter Zone. Tanyl explained once that Starter Zone NPCs are aware of the outside world so they can help Players acclimate to the Realms. They know that the Hydrologists created the Realms and the quests. So they must understand that the barn they are compelled to build burns down every few months. And the process begins again. Looped. No end in sight.

I'm surprised they don't turn on players en masse.

Outside of the Starter Zone, though, Tanyl told us the NPCs don't know about any world except the Realms. Perhaps they have a different perspective.

Except for the enslaved humans. They certainly know the living nightmare they are going through each day. I wonder if they talk to the computer-generated NPCs. I wonder if those beings would believe the truth if they were told.

Alby and I came so close to that fate when we were forcefully inscribed. If not for the password supplied by Michael ... my brain refuses to continue that train of thought.

I have to tread very carefully. One misstep now in MidWorld could condemn us to NPC slave status for all eternity.

# Chapter Seven

"The changes that you make to your Homestead are permanent," Darlene explains. "When you cut down a tree, for example, it's not going to regrow. You'll need to plant another tree. If you dig out an area for a mine, the ore nodes will not respawn like they do in the Realms. You'll have a permanent hole in the earth."

"But we can bring in materials from outside to build our homes?"

"Of course. And you can replace items from your Homestead. To continue with the example, the trees can be grown from seeds. And the growth rate is at the same speed as in the Realms."

"I don't understand." My brow furrows. "The plants, vegetables, and flowers we picked seemed to grow back overnight."

"A lot of the crops do grow that quickly. Some take longer. And, of course, some only grow in the Realms. But the trees take a few days to grow. I think it averages out day-to-year. So if a type of tree in our former world would reach its full growth in 60 years, it takes 60 days in the Realms and on your Homestead."

"Will we need a gauntlet for each of us?"

"It's soul-bound to the user. So you'll want one ... uh two more? They are a thousand gold a piece."

Two thousand gold. Wow. But we do have the money for it. And having the three of us able to work on our Homestead will be more efficient.

"Please." I smile.

Darlene makes another notation on her tablet. "With this you need to give specific permissions to your sister and to L.G. so they can modify your Homestead."

"Absolutely. We should all have equal rights."

"Well, the Founder will always be able to determine another Homestead resident's rights. But I can put both of them in the next tier category. And that will give the, um, hodag a few extra perks usually reserved for players, like the ability to use a bag for storage. Once you finalize that, they will be all set."

"Sounds good." I'm not sure what she's talking about, but I want everyone to be equal. Or as equal as we can be. And it will be helpful if L.G. can carry stuff in his own bag.

"Do you want to purchase a bank box?"

"What is that?" I ask.

"It's a special chest that gives you direct access to your family bank. That way you can put items into the bank, or remove them, without having to visit a town. It's a 5 thousand gold add-on, but I think it's worth it simply for the convenience factor."

Okay, that makes the bill 7 thousand gold so far. It's still within our budget. "Sounds good."

She taps on her tablet. "One final decision before you can get started. You get one free pattern and materials for your Homestead. A small two-story building designed in the Realm One aesthetic."

"Aesthetic?" I bet she used that word on purpose, knowing I wouldn't understand.

"Designed like the homes you've seen in Old Town. Farmhouses. Cottages. Stone and wood. Post and beam construction. Timber frames." She waves her hand at the screen and hundreds of tiny pictures of dwellings appeared. "You don't get much with the base pattern, but you can add on later. Most people use their first pattern to practice building. Learn how to work a gauntlet. That sort of thing. They almost never live in those buildings for long."

The buildings look nice to me. They are slightly larger than the homes that fill Old Town and the surrounding area. The third one to the left, a two-story building called a Queen's Post Saltbox, looks like it might be simple to build. And it's made of stone with wood accents. It looks sturdy. "Do people need that much room? Do they have large families or something?"

"It goes back to what you were used to in the real world and in the Aquariums. And of course, the more you develop your Homestead, the more Prestige Points you accumulate."

Prestige Points? I haven't heard about those before. I open my mouth to ask, but she doesn't halt her spiel.

"You don't need to downgrade here, Cami. The world is your oyster. The only limit is your imagination!"

And my bank account, I think, but I don't say that out loud.

"Could we live in a tree like Tanyl?" Alby asks.

"Absolutely, my dear." Darlene waves her hand and pulls up another screen. "There are dozens of tree house patterns starting at only 20 thousand gold. Of course, if you want something truly special, you can work with a designer. That's a bit more expensive, I'm afraid. But what is cost compared to living in the home of your wildest dreams?"

"How many house patterns are there?"

She looks at her tablet. "Right now for Realm One there are one million building patterns. And 10 million patterns for fixtures and furnishings."

"Do we have to upgrade today?" I have to put the brakes on this. Our money is limited, but I don't want Darlene to know. We're supposed to be wealthy players used to absolute luxury. "I'm anxious to see our Homestead and experiment with the gauntlet. The Queen's Post Saltbox looks like a nice building to start with, and we can discuss building something additional in the future.

There are so many patterns, it will be hard to choose."

"Of course. You can get settled in and come back to look through the catalogs." She taps her tablet. "I've put a notation that you are allowed to return and browse whenever you wish. When you make a purchase, though, you'll need to work with a Hydrologist." She smiles. "I hope you will ask for me."

Fat chance I'll be coming back here. I can't wait to get away. And why does she want to help us? She must be getting something in return. A commission I would guess. But I simply smile and say nothing.

"Here we go." She finishes tapping on her tablet. "All you have to do is sign your full name where I've indicated with the yellow arrow and we'll be good to go."

I take the tablet and stylus. Wow. So much tiny print. This will take hours to read.

"No reason to go through the forms, dear. What we've discussed has been recorded. For your protection, and for mine." Darlene breaks out her salesperson grin and points to a small half-dome of glass on the ceiling. "Big Brother's always watching." She laughs at her own joke.

I had suspected we were being observed. This confirms my fear. "Oh." I try to sound non-committal.

"And I added a free bonus in there just for signing today. A bedroom furniture set to get you started."

"Can I get a copy of this?"

"I'll make sure a copy is mailed to you in-Realm. No worries."

No time like the present, I guess. It's not like the world is going to end when I sign my name. I write "Camille Malifux" with a flourish and hand Darlene the tablet.

A siren blares. After a moment, the lights begin to pulse in sync with the alarm.

# Chapter Eight

"What's happening?" I'm on my feet standing next to Alby and L.G.

Darlene shakes her head. "I'm not sure ..." Her voice trails off as she begins opening screens on her tablet.

The sound of the alarm grates against my ears. After so many months in the peace and quiet of the Realms, it's loud enough to be physically painful. Alby slams the palms of her hands against her ears to deaden the sound. L.G. shakes his head in pain. I reach down and cover his ears with my own hands.

"Turn off the alarm." I yell over the din.

"I'm trying!" Strain shows on her face. "Ah, there we go." The noise level decreases as she enters something into the tablet. "I can't turn it off, but I managed to turn it down."

A chill slips over my skin as I straighten up. Alby lowers her hands and reaches over to hug L.G. I can tell by the way her arm tightens around him that she feels as uneasy as I do.

"Ow," he says, shaking his head. He glares at Darlene, probably blaming her for the noise.

"Are we in danger?" I ask. "Is the building on fire?"

"No, it's not that." She frowns and taps on the screen. "It's an intruder alert. But that can't be. No one can get into MidWorld without our knowledge."

"If it's impossible, then why would you install an alarm in the first place?"

"Um ... Good question." Darlene taps on her screen some more. I have a feeling she isn't really listening. "Girls I've got to go and check this out. Stay here until someone comes for you."

"No." My voice is firm.

Alby and L.G. look at me, their eyes wide. I shake my head faintly and concentrate on our group connection, urging them to keep quiet and to follow my lead.

"No?" Darlene repeats, startled.

"I don't know anyone here, aside from you, Susan, and Mr. Harrisburg. If there is an intruder, how would I know? We're sticking with you."

Thankfully Darlene accepts this reasoning. "Okay, but stay close to me. If I tell you to run, head back to this room."

Assuming we can find it, I think, but I don't say anything out loud other than "okay."

We follow her out into the corridor. She collides with someone else, falling to the ground and dropping her tablet. It skids to my feet. I pick it up before it can be kicked away. Another Hydrologist bumps my hand and I almost drop the tablet. I instinctively put it in my bag to keep it safe.

Darlene climbs to her feet. "Manners people!" she mutters beneath her breath. "No one should be in that much of a rush."

A stream of Hydrologists in white lab coats push us along behind her. They look like animals fleeing before a forest fire. I wrap one arm around Alby and the other around L.G. I don't want to become separated. We weave past a clot of Hydrologists who stand near a screen and watch pastel-colored blobs shift and transform shape.

I have no idea what information they can glean from the blobs, but one of them points to an irregular shape. Others peer at the screen. They start gesturing wildly.

I look closely as we pass. I'm right. It's a blob. A peach-and-rose colored blob.

Technology in MidWorld is weird.

"What have they found?" I ask Darlene.

She shrugs. "It's not important. A system is on the blink. We'll get it fixed. It's nothing for you to worry about."

She's lying, of course. I can sense it. I'm sure Alby and L.G. realize it too. Maybe sticking with her isn't such a hot idea. But it's the only option we have right now.

There's an explosion in the distance. The floor shudders beneath my feet. Voices scream. I'm almost surprised that my voice isn't one of the jagged chorus. But I've been expecting something like this. It's important to remain calm. Screaming does no one any good. And it might frighten Alby and L.G., who are taking this in stride because I am.

The siren comes back at full strength. A skein of bitter, acrid smoke drifts down from the vents near the ceiling. One of the grilles blow off and shoots across the corridor like a projectile.

"Come on!" Darlene says, opening a door to a stairwell. "I've got to get you out of here. It's more than my job's worth."

What does she mean? Will she be in trouble if we're hurt? Or if we see something that we shouldn't? What could they do to her? What could they do to us?

And, come to think of it, who are "they?" The other Hydrologists? Is there a CEO of some sort? Or a board of directors? I've lived in the Realms for months and it's amazing how little I know about the people in charge. None of that seemed to matter until now. And I don't think this is a good time to ask these questions.

We pound down a flight of steel stairs, our footsteps mingling with the monotonous drilling beat of the alarm, and hurry along a narrow corridor. She opens a door and we enter a room filled with seemingly endless isles of desks covered with computers and other electronic equipment. Indirect lighting glows from panels placed high along the walls.

"I'll get your Homestead package and then you can use the portal to go to your new home."

We look curiously at the deserted computer workstations while Darlene walks over to a terminal and pulls up a new screen. She enters some information and frowns as the power flickers.

"No, you stupid thing. Three gauntlets!"

"Does yelling at it help?" I ask.

"No, but thumping it sometimes does." The screen flashes and she raps it on the side with the palm of her hand. The picture stabilizes. A stainless-steel panel in the wall slides open, revealing a square of darkness. Something sparkly flashes within it. A box seemingly made of blue light flares into being. Darlene picks it up and hands it to me.

"Here you go. This has all of the items for your Homestead, plus the add-ons you've purchased."

I take it and put it in my bag. My mind still boggles at the fact that such a small container could hold all of those items. That right now I'm carrying an entire house in my bag.

No matter what term people use—magic or technology—this is a pretty impressive trick.

"Okay. I need to program the information for your Homestead address now." She gestures for us to move closer and picks up a large, glowing tube. "I need a bit of DNA from you Cami. Just a small prick of the finger. It locks your ownership of the Homestead and temporarily links this portal so you can travel there."

She smiles a bit and holds up the tube. I know it probably won't hurt much, but I've never liked it when a nurse drew my blood at the doctor's office. And Darlene isn't a nurse. How much medical training does she have?

I remind myself that doing this quickly will mean we can get out of MidWorld that much faster. I offer up my hand and tense as she pulls a cap off of the tube, revealing a needle.

I don't want to watch her jab my finger and turn my head away. Something catches my eye, a shadow of movement behind one of the ventilator grills near the ceiling, and I don't even feel it when the needle breaks through my skin.

"There now. Almost finished." Darlene turns back to the computer screen, tapping out commands. "This portal is special. It links to all of the Homestead portals. But the address is keyed to your DNA. So no one will be able to go to your Homestead except you and the people you give permission."

My eyes drift back to the ventilator grill. What I saw there before wasn't my imagination. A face, high cheekbones, thick eyelashes, with dark hair badly in need of a haircut, floats behind the cream-colored louvers.

I recognize the young man I rescued before I was grabbed by the military and forcefully inscribed. The one who gave me the password "Friends and Family" that enabled me to scam my way into the game. To be inscribed as a Player, as a Founder, instead of an NPC slave.

Michael—who betrayed me. Who promised to help search the hospital compound for Alby, but left as soon as we came across an exit.

So it's a mixed bag of both good and bad. I'm not angry enough to betray his presence to the Hydrologists, and I'm not thankful enough to try and help him.

He's obviously been inscribed as a human. He looks just like he did in our former world. And he's hiding in the vents, crawling around inside the MidWorld complex for goodness knows what purpose.

He could have a reason for crawling through the vents, spying on the Hydrologists. He could have a perfectly good reason.

Yeah, right.

I wonder if he recognizes me? I know I've changed. A lot. Blue face. Silver hair. Pointy ears. But my face looks the same. And, of course, I still have freckles.

"Remember to set your **Residence Stones** to your Homestead after you construct your house. Otherwise you will have to come back here to enter your Homestead again."

**Residence Stones** are the type of magic I like in the Realms. They can be used at any distance. We could wander the Realms all day and be home almost instantly.

"But L.G. doesn't have a **Residence Stone**," Alby says.

"He does now. There's one included in the package I gave Cami, along with an **Invisible Bag** so he can carry items without changing his appearance."

"Cool," I say, and I mean it. People who think up things like **Residence Stones** and **Invisible Bags** can't be all bad. Can they?

"Time to go, Cami, Alby, and um ... L.G." The salesperson grin is stretched on Darlene's face again. I think it galls her to acknowledge L.G. and that emotion is at war with her desire to keep me happy and spending money.

"When you go through the door over there," she says, pointing to a secure door at the far end of the room, "you'll find a portal to your Homestead. You can take all the time that you need to get set up. And when you want to buy something else for your Homestead, don't forget to ask for me. I'm always happy to help."

At our approach a small wall panel opens to reveal a palm print reader. A computer-generated AI speaks up, sounding like a friendly man's voice. "Please provide DNA verification."

I press my hand against the pressure pad.

"DNA verification confirmed."

The security door slides open. The blue light of a portal fills the small room.

"Go on," I say to L.G. and Alby.

"Don't jump," L.G. reminds me as he prepares to step through.

"I won't." I smile.

"Good luck! And remember, Cami, you can have whatever you desire. The only limit is your imagination." Darlene gives a small wave and turns back to the computer terminal. She enters some information and the door starts to close.

"Oh, wait, I have your tablet!" I say, holding it up, but it's too late. She doesn't hear before the door shuts.

But someone does. Michael's eyes lock on me and they narrow. Even if he hadn't recognized me before, Darlene yelling my name probably jogged his memory.

Is he interested in me, or in the tablet? Or both?

I've never been the type of person who can predict change coming in her life. I just try to go on the best way I know how. Avoiding problems. Protecting my family. Making plans to steer clear of disaster. Having those plans go awry. Fixing the results. Moving forward.

From the intensity of Michael's look, prediction is easy this time. I know that life is about to smack me in the face.

# Chapter Nine

**W**arning. You are entering
*Homestead 14508. Realm One.*
*Registered Owner: Camille Malifux.*
*Proceed: Yes/No.*

"Yes." The last sparkle of light has barely
faded from the portal. I'm still trying to get my
bearings.

"What should we do first?" My sister
bounces in place, ready to explore our new
home. L.G. quivers in excitement as well. I'm
surprised they waited for me before taking off
to explore.

This is how far we've come in the Realms.
How comfortable we feel. Back in our old
lives, it never would have crossed my mind
that Alby would go anywhere without me. Or
that she might venture off into something new
without making sure I was there to hold her
hand and keep her safe.

Now, she's growing up. She and L.G. watch out for each other. They feel safe venturing out on their own in the Realms.

I'm the one having trouble letting go.

I wish I had someone to talk to about all of this. But Alby and L.G. are too young. I need someone older. Someone who I can exchange ideas with. Someone who can provide a different perspective. Because stumbling around does not seem like the wisest thing in the world. But right now all I have are my own thoughts and the advice my dad gave me. And he would say that worrying doesn't take away your troubles. Anxiety destroys your peace.

I could spend the next few hours thinking about Michael, figuring out the implications of his presence in MidWorld. But I don't have time. I can't focus on my thoughts, on my fears, and also enjoy the moment and the discovery of our new Homestead. As dad used to say, make your plans for tomorrow, but don't forget to experience the joy of today.

And right now keeping Alby and L.G. happy are more important than worrying about Michael. I'll have time to deal with him later.

"Let's map it out. See our new home. Look for a nice place to build the house. Someplace where the ground is flat."

"Maybe near the lake?"

"Yeah, but not too close. We don't know about the weather yet." I look up into the clear blue sky. "Or flooding. Or mosquitoes."

"There are no mosquitoes, silly. The Hydrologists wouldn't put those into the Realms."

"You sound very sure of yourself. There are butterflies. And spiders," I counter. "Why not other creepy crawlies?"

"I've read more than you. In Tanyl's library. No mosquitoes, gnats, or flies."

"Oh, well, then, it must be true if it's in a book," I tease her.

"Uh huh."

"Yep," L.G. says. "Books are true."

"I bow before the logic of the two experts in our group," I say. They both giggle. "I can't wait to have our own library." The idea of snuggling up in front of a fire each night with a book and a cup of hot chocolate sounds heavenly.

"We need a place for a garden, too." Alby pulls out the **Flying Carpet** and sets it up so that L.G. can ride on it. We both shift to **Flight Form**.

"We can figure out how to plant all those seeds we collected." I pat my **Bag of Infinite Holding** for emphasis.

"Cami?"

"Yeah."

"Can we have a tree house someday?"

"Maybe. We need to earn some money first, though. Before we buy anything new from the Hydrologists."

"Okay. I kinda thought so. We weren't rich before, right?"

"No. That's not something you should talk about though. With anyone outside our family."

"I won't."

"Me either." L.G. says.

"Why is it important?" I ask.

"Other players talk about it. How much gold they have. What they did before they were inscribed."

"If you have to brag about all the material stuff in your life, there probably isn't much substance to it."

"Yeah."

"You don't say anything, though, right?"

"No. I don't. I remember what dad said."

Dad's rules keep us safe. After the world went to heck-in-a-handbasket, he shared them every day. Never talk to anyone about your personal life. People want to know things, but it's never because they are just curious. They want to learn about your weaknesses. To learn where you have stashed food. Or clean water.

They want to learn about you so they can take what's yours.

"I don't want to go back to MidWorld. Even if it means getting a tree house." Alby frowns. "It's safe here. It's scary there."

"It's too noisy in MidWorld, and the people are mean," L.G. says in his gravely voice.

"It's like with all those noises there, you don't know what's happening."

"Yeah," he agrees. "It gave me a headache."

"Something could come around the corner. And something could happen."

L.G. nods in agreement. I'm having trouble following her logic.

"What do you mean?"

"Some sounds you can imagine what happened and in real life that thing did not happen, but if you imagine it, you think about what could happen."

"Yeah," L.G. says.

"So it's scary because you can't see it, but you can imagine it." I think for a minute. "I can understand that. But sometimes I think the things you do see are scarier than anything you can imagine."

"I have a really good imagination." Alby nods her head so fast her braids bounce on her shoulders.

"Me too," L.G. adds.

"Well, we're safe here. And it's quiet." We sit still for a moment, listening. The wind gently ruffles through the trees. The water splashes around rocks in the stream. "I think we're lucky to be here."

"We're lucky that dad paid for our lives in the Realms."

"Yes, we are." The lie comes more easily now. Slips past my lips without a pause or hesitation. We are safer if neither one of them knows the truth. After what happened today I'm even more convinced that I need to carry this burden on my own.

The fact that it's the right decision doesn't make me feel any better about lying to the ones I love.

Alby takes wing and L.G. and I follow her. Our Homestead is beautiful from above. Green fields and trees, blue sparkling water bubbling over rocks and stones, white sand on a beach near the lake.

But the things that are missing strike me the most. There are no wildflowers in the meadows. In the Starter Zone, there are so many bluebells, foxgloves, daffodils, violets, lilies and a profusion of other flowers that it can sometimes be hard to see the green grass. And each flower, while beautiful, has specific properties. They are used in food or, more likely, in potion-making. Alby, L.G. and I have hundreds of thousands of flowers stored in the bank and have gathered seeds as well. The seeds drop randomly, about 2 or 3 for every 100 flowers or vegetables picked. We have enough gathered to start our own farm.

It's empty. We decide how it will be filled. I shiver with anticipation. This is a good use of my imagination. Instead of focusing on fears, focus on potential.

To see the world in a grain of sand ... A fragment of a poem I heard a long time ago, probably when I was in school, drifts through my mind. I can't remember the rest. Somehow it fits our new Homestead, though.

The Homesteads are like Alby's sand art projects. The basic outline is there, but the artist needs to place each grain of sand in order to develop the perfect work of art. Here, the three of us get to place all of the materials that change the framework of a Homestead into a masterpiece. Into our home.

I float a bit higher, the wind lifting me to the level of the clouds.

*Warning. You are approaching the upper level barrier of Homestead 14508. Reverse course.*

"What happens if I cross the boundary?" I ask the AI.

*Considering: Players cannot cross Homestead boundaries. They are solid, although invisible, barriers. The only way to cross the boundary is with a Registered Portal or a linked Residence Stone.*

But it's not completely invisible. I can see the air rippling in tiny visible waves, distorting the wispy trail of a cloud passing through the sky. The pattern is curved slightly, which means that we are in a protective bubble like a snow globe.

I shift course and fly level with Alby and L.G. I give them the information shared by the AI. This is one time that I hope the AI continues to give warnings. I don't want to fly head-first into an almost invisible wall.

"You think it's just like a ring of bubbles around the outside of MidWorld and the Realms?" Alby asks.

"Sounds right based on what Darlene said."

"I wonder what's in the gaps."

"In-between the Homesteads?"

"If they're round, like bubbles, they won't fit together. There will be gaps."

"Spaces in-between," I say. "I don't know."

"Sounds scary." She shivers.

"Could be monsters," L.G. says.

"Or it could be pudding." I make a face and they both laugh. Since we're still in **Flight Form** Alby's laugh sounds like a series of caws. "And since it could be anything, I'm voting for pudding."

"I vote for frosting." L.G. grins.

"Okay. I change my vote. Frosting it is."

Although I've managed to keep this on a light note, Alby's comments remind me that there is so much about our new world I don't know. So much about how it all works I don't understand.

Back when we first arrived in the Realms, we encountered an area where players were not meant to travel. It was an area in-between the Starter Zone and an outdoor raid. In-between two of the bubbles, so to speak. The AI stopped working. It wouldn't identify the spider-like creatures that lived in the tunnel.

Was that one of the gaps? And if something could live there, like the spiders, could there be monsters in-between?

# Chapter Ten

"So what's the first step?" Alby asks after we finish touring the boundaries of our Homestead and pick an area to build on. We choose a small hilltop overlooking the lake. It's relatively free of trees and bushes and is somewhat flat. A clearing not too far away will be perfect for a garden.

"I guess I should open the package Darlene gave me." I take the box seemingly made of blue light out of my **Bag of Infinite Holding** and open it. What looks like a pile of irregularly shaped crates spill out onto the grass and stack up at our feet.

"Wow!" I can't believe all of that fit into such a small space. But it's a whole house. I have to keep that in mind.

"It's like Christmas! Look." Alby points to a box. "That one has my name on it."

"Well, unwrap it." I can't help smiling. They're not really wrapped, but I have to go along with the holiday theme. I find one with my name and a slightly larger one for L.G.

"On three." We open the boxes at the same time. They disappear without a trace. The AI is stuttering as it tries to keep up with announcing what we find. Basically all three of us now have **Gauntlets** and L.G. has his **Residence Stone** and an **Invisible Bag**. That bag is impressive. It has 100 slots and no weight limit.

"It looks good on you," Alby says with a straight face. He arches an eyebrow at her.

The **Gauntlets** cover our right hands all the way to the elbow. They are made of metal, silver, and brass, and sparkle in the sunlight.

The rest of the boxes beckon, but they are labeled with numbers, not with names. I choose the box labeled "One" and pry it open.

The box melts away, revealing a square white block with a blue light pulsing in the center. I pick it up and the AI chimes in with information.

*Congratulations! You have discovered a* **Cornerstone**.

*You have learned the **Building Skill**. Current level: 1*

*Review: Yes or No?*

"Yes."

The **Building Skill** allows players and enhanced NPCs to create buildings on a Homestead. Each **Cornerstone** provides a Blueprint, or Building Plan, of a prefabricated structure. This Blueprint provides an overlay in order to help erect the structures by suggesting the exact position of specific building materials.

Players can change the design of the structure and substitute building materials during the construction process. Blueprints are suggestions, after all, and are mainly designed to make building structures easier. Be creative.

Quest Offered: **A Ground-Breaking Quest.**

Difficulty Level: 2.

Reward: Increased Abilities and Knowledge. Yes or No?

"Yes." The three of us answer together. I place the cornerstone down on the ground where we chose to erect the house.

The building appears. Or, rather, a shadow of it appears outlined in white.

"Cool." Alby walks into the pattern, and we follow her. The structure can be seen, but faintly, like the floor and walls are constructed of light.

I trip over a rock and pitch forward. "Careful," I say, catching my balance. "It may look like the floor is here, but we're walking on the grass."

"What do we do now?" Alby spins around. "How do we get started putting it together?"

There are some areas outlined in red. Places where the ground is not completely level. "Maybe we have to remove those areas before we can build the rest."

L.G. points his **Gauntlet** at the ground. The soil, grass, and rocks tremble and then erupt upward, flowing toward his **Gauntlet** in a slow-moving fountain. Pretty soon the red outline of the pattern disappears, and the blueprint is completely outlined in white.

"Where did the stuff go? The grass and dirt?" I ask.

"In my new bag." He frowns. "I got it all dirty."

"I think we might need that dirt to fill in some of the spaces around the foundation," I say. "Don't worry. I don't think the dirt will be in your bag for long."

We open the boxes in order, finding stone and wood. Placing the materials with the **Gauntlets** is simple. The process reminds me of building houses made of toy blocks when I was a child. But here the process seems to be permanent.

Once the foundation and flooring are laid, the supportive structures flow into place. Wooden beams and wooden interior walls, stone outer walls, frames for windows, glass panes that snap into place, a fireplace and field-stone chimney, and neatly scaled slate roofing tiles. All told it takes us about an hour to construct the house. Everything is complete except for the furnishings.

We take a break for lunch before tackling the interior. I've brought two tomato sandwiches and a big salad for L.G. By unspoken agreement we eat outside, resting on green grass as thick as a carpet. Our first official meal in our new home should be special. But in reality we will probably end up eating leftover pieces of Alby's birthday cake before falling asleep tonight.

Life is life, after all. No matter what Darlene says, it's not all fantasy. Maybe some people can afford to just drift through this portion of the Realms and have NPCs do all the building, but what fun is that?

Building something here isn't that different than our former world. There you also had blueprints and used items from the world around you to make a house. True, most people hired professionals to build houses or, more tellingly, bought pre-built homes. But I remember seeing people build homes in my neighborhood. It seemed like fun. At least when the weather was good.

"Dad will like this house," Alby says. "Do you think we'll see him soon?" She takes another bite of sandwich.

The pain slices through me, like someone has stabbed me in the chest. No one has, of course, but the pain is so real I put my hand on my heart for a moment. "Alby, dad is dead. We talked about this, remember?"

"Yeah." She drops her head. "It's just...everyone rezes here. People don't stay dead. I thought that maybe..." her voice trails off.

"He died in the other world. Our former world. People don't rez there. They stay dead."

"I just hope." Her eyes well up and tears travel down her face. "I wish…" L.G. snuggles next to her and I pull them both into a big hug.

"Shhh, it's okay. Don't worry. Don't worry."

Maybe it had been a mistake, not letting her see him ... after. But the Hydrologist that took over his body was strong. Articulate. Persuasive. After he infected dad he almost convinced me to let him go. That if I helped him, he would leave my dad's body. That everything would go back to normal. If I just gave him everything he wanted.

Yeah, right.

I could have let him go. But that's not what dad wanted. Alby was too young in his opinion for this type of talk, but he prepared me for a scenario where one of us had been infected by inscribed water. He made me promise, made me swear, on my love for him, on my love for my sister, that I would follow through if the inscribed water permanently took over his mind.

I keep my promises.

Tears fill my eyes. I blink hard to keep them from spilling down my face. "It's been a big day. We're tired. Let's just set up the furniture that Darlene gave us and call it a day. "

"Can we build a fire?"

"Sure." I smile. "There's a fireplace in the living room and in the big bedroom upstairs. Where do you want to build it?"

"In the bedroom. So we can watch it while we go to sleep."

"Sounds good."

"We're going to share a room?"

"For now. There are three bedrooms so we can all have our own rooms if you want."

"We've always shared a room." She wrinkles her nose. "I think it would be scary to sleep alone."

"Yeah," says L.G.

"Hey! Whether we're in the same room or not, we're together. We're family." I place a kiss on each of their foreheads. "Come on. Let's find some dead branches for our fire."

"It's too bad the crates disappear." Alby says. "That thin wood would make good kindling."

"Ah well, maybe they recycle the boxes."

"Magic recycling?"

"Mmm hmm."

"That's silly." She reaches over and taps me on the arm. "Tag, you're it. Come on L.G. Scatter!" They rush off.

"Don't forget to look for dead branches!" I call out. It still amazes me how fast her moods can change. I probably was the same when I was eight.

But something bothers me about the conversation. I have a feeling that she doesn't quite believe me that dad won't be coming back. It's hard to accept something when your eyes show you the exact opposite every day. When your heart wants something impossible to be true.

I don't know how to bring up my doubts without upsetting her further. And there have already been enough tears shed on her birthday. So I figuratively bite my tongue and chase into the woods after them.

# Chapter Eleven

Quest Complete! *A Ground-Breaking Quest.*
Reward: Building Experience and Knowledge.
Building Skill: Current Level 2
Congratulations Player! You have earned 100 Prestige Points for adding a building to your Homestead.
Current Homestead 14508 Prestige Points: 100

The AI chimes in after we finish setting up the portals, the fabricator, and the forge in one of the two front rooms on the lower level. I also put our bank box, which looks like a large wooden chest, in that room. That way we will have access to the materials in the bank when we want to build or create something new. It's also not too far from the kitchen.

"We're going to have to get a stove," I say to Alby.

"Yeah, and a lot of other stuff. But not a refrigerator."

"Nope." That's another nice aspect of food in the realms. If the items are in our bags, or in the bank, food doesn't spoil.

The rooms feel extraordinarily empty and echo when we talk. Only two rooms have any furniture. The Portal Room and the Master Bedroom, where we installed Darlene's furniture set, consisting of a four-poster, king-size bed, long white curtains, two padded chairs in a light tan fabric, and an ottoman. The bed appeared right from the box made up with white linens, a tan throw blanket, and an extremely large blue and white accent pillow. It almost fills the room. Last night we practiced moving it around with the gauntlets until we found the perfect position between the windows. Alby and I shared the bed while L.G. curled up on a pillow right in front of the fireplace.

They both fell asleep right away. It took me awhile to drift off, but I didn't want to sneak off to the Training Center and leave them alone. Not during our first night in our new home. So I tossed and turned and my slumbers were filled with disturbing dreams. The gentle, kind face of my father intertwined with the hate-filled grimace of the Hydrologist who took over his body, with Alby thin and starving as we ran from the looter gangs. With L.G. being stalked by those mutant spiders, falling into their web, with no rescue in sight. I woke up over and over, needing to reassure myself that they were fine. Only after seeing them in the faint light of the fire taking the deep breaths of slumber let me relax. That relief lasted until the next round of nightmares pulled me awake, drenched in a cold sweat.

"You look tired." L.G. says, dragging me back to the present moment.

"I never sleep well in a new place. I'll get used to it, though."

"It's a good place. Lots of green."

"Maybe that's why you two feel at home. But I'm blue, not green."

"So we need to plant some flowers for you. Blue ones." Alby grins. "And make some blue furniture for you at the school."

"There's a furniture-making profession? I don't remember reading about that."

"No, but every profession can make things to furnish a house. And there is a woodworking profession. That deals with a lot of the furniture patterns."

"Really?"

"Mmhmm."

"Well you two will just have to get busy."

A small "ding" sounds outside the front door. We rush through the doorway, curious to see what made the noise.

A small, silver mailbox has appeared next to the door. Since it wasn't there last night, the house completion must have triggered its appearance.

It is glowing blue, indicating that there are letters.

*You have mail.*

My only message is the Homestead contract/bill of sale Darlene had promised to send. I stick it in my bag to read later.

"I got my enrollment information from the professions school," Alby says.

"Me too." L.G. holds his up proudly.

"What's it say?" I crane my neck, trying to read over her shoulder, but I needn't have bothered. The AI supplies the information.

*Professionum Scholae*
*Headmaster: Professor Didicit,*

*Wizard of the First Realm, Grand Master Crafter and Inventor, and Co-Chair of the Council of Thirteen*

*Dear Ms. Malifux,*

*At the Professionum Scholae we seek individuals who demonstrate competence, character, and purpose, those who aspire to possess skills every bit as valuable as swordplay or spell craft. The Realm needs creative and talented individuals. We believe that you possess these traits.*

*Congratulations! I am delighted to offer you admission to the Professionum Scholae class of 04.*

*The Professionum Scholae will provide you the opportunity to expand your knowledge within a community of diverse and deeply engaged students and faculty members. Here you will find training in Alchemy, Blacksmithing, Cooking, Farming, Jewel Crafting, Leather Working, Tailoring, Tinkering, Weapon Smithing, and Woodcrafting. I am confident that you will find the Professionum Scholae experience to be some of the most challenging and rewarding years of your life.*

*Financial Requirements*

*Tuition is waived for all members of a Homestead.*

*Every admitted student is responsible for either purchasing or providing the necessary materials and equipment to level a profession.*

*Please find enclosed a list of all necessary materials and equipment for each profession. Note: You do not need to register for all of the professions at once. Students are encouraged to learn one profession at time.*

*Your Next Steps*

*Return the confirmation card included in your admission packet.*

*On behalf of the faculty and staff of Professionum Scholae, please accept my warmest congratulations.*

*Yours Sincerely,*

*Jemma Depraysie,*

*Deputy Headmistress*

"There's a list that goes with it." Alby hands it to me.

List? It's almost thick enough to be a book. Each profession is included, starting with Alchemy, and has thousands of items required for leveling along with prices. The numbers swim before my eyes. The amount of gold needed to level only one profession is staggering. There's no way we can afford this.

"Cami?" My little sister's eyes are wide. "Are you okay?" She and L.G. look alarmed.

I can't disappoint them. But how am I going to be able to afford this?

"It's just a lot of money." My voice quavers. "I didn't realize it would cost so much."

"That's why Tanyl suggested we start with Alchemy. L.G. and I can share the Alchemist Table and use all of the flowers and herbs we picked in the Starter Zone to make the low-level potions and elixirs." She looks at me. "You can use it too, you know, when you want to start training."

Right. "I remember talking about that with him."

"And since you're going out to explore the other Zones, you can get us the rest of the flowers and herbs as you level up."

"Right." Crisis averted. Sort of. "It might take a while."

She shrugs. "Tanyl says they have a really good library at the school. So we'll be able to 'Read. Improve our minds' when we're not in class." She giggles as she says his favorite phrase.

"And eat cookies," L.G. waggles his eyebrows.

"Yeah," Alby looks over the list I'm holding. "Can we sign up for Cooking too? We can buy the Gourmet Stove and be able to do all of the simple low-level recipes with the fruits and veggies we've picked as well as the advanced recipes in the future."

"I think that's a good idea." Each unit costs 10 thousand gold. Holy guacamole! That will eat up most of our savings. But it will help keep them occupied until they are of age to explore the rest of the realms. Help them flourish and improve their minds. And we won't have dipped into the single platinum coin yet, so it will continue to earn interest. There's that.

Still, it's back to me heading out and providing for my family like I did before we joined the Realms. Instead of scavenging for food and supplies in burned-out buildings while hiding from looter gangs, I'll be exploring the zones. Gathering the materials they will need to continue their education. Earning money from completing quests to support us.

It's as good of a plan as I can come up with in the situation. I hate the fact that it's so vague, that I have to build all of our lives from mere hope, the flimsiest of materials.

There aren't many props holding up our world. If even one cracks, everything can come tumbling down.

# Chapter Twelve

After setting our **Residence Stones** to our Homestead, we travel through the only open portal. It places us at the edge of Starter Zone, near enough to Old Town that we can see the buildings in the distance, and close to the invisible border between the zones.

We fly to Tanyl's residence and he helps me complete the registration for Alby and L.G. The four of us go through the two-way portal for the school that is set up in a secluded grove outside of Tinker's Town and arrive at the Professionum Scholae Campus.

The portal opens into a garden outside the main buildings. The fragrances from the cultivated flowers provide a rich scent and the colors from the blooms against the pebble-pressed stone walls look almost like stained-glass.

"Can we have a garden like this?" Alby asks. Her brown eyes shine with awe and excitement.

"Yes, I think we can." My lips curve in a smile. I can picture working on it at the Homestead. I recognize few of the flowers, though, and would love to learn more about them.

The main campus is even more impressive. Graceful white stone towers reach skyward, their apexes blue encircled with a red-tinted cedar-type wood balconies. Radiant, blue-and-white hovering stones dance around them, providing illumination. There was ivy here too, almost obscuring the small windows.

We head down a flagstone path. The iron-bar gates disappear as we walk toward them. More evidence of magic.

A middle-aged NPC stands in the gateway. She has thick wheat-golden hair done up in a braid that goes to her waist. Her eyes are a warm brown with smile-crinkles in the corner. She's taller than a dwarf, but shorter than a human. Just about a head shorter than Alby.

*Jemma Depraysie,*

*Deputy Headmistress of the Professionum Scholae*

*Level 20*

*Race: Droll*

*Alignment: Neutral*

"Droll?" Alby whispers.

I shake my head.

"Half-dwarf, half-troll," Tanyl says. "Pay attention now."

"There you are then, Miss Malifux. Mr. Hodag. I'm Professor Depraysie. Follow me please."

They walk in. I try to follow, but Professor Depraysie holds up her hand. "Students, faculty, and staff only, Ms. Malifux. It's a closed campus when classes are in session. No visitors allowed except by special permission. It's one of the ways we keep our students safe."

"You two feeling okay here?" I ask. Both Alby and L.G. nod.

"Watch out for each other. And don't leave our group. Keep in contact. If something happens, use the **Residence Stones** and I'll meet you back home."

"Okay, Cami."

"You betcha," L.G. says, bringing a smile to my face.

Pangs of unease squeeze my belly as they walk away. Not that I'm worried about the school. I had toured the campus a few weeks ago with Tanyl when it was shut down between terms. We didn't use the portals for traveling. We took the long way around on the path from Old Town to Tinker's Town.

Being connected to the Starter Zone, the area is safe. The same rules and restrictions to protect younger players apply. It's just that we've been together for years. I watched out for Alby since the day she was born. And L.G., he's like a little brother. Now they are going off and having adventures without me. And I'll be alone.

Well, expect for Tanyl.

"Come with me, now. It is time for you to begin your training in the fae's magical abilities. You will need to choose your next trainer." He spins and heads back toward the two-way portal in the garden.

"You don't oversee that training?" I ask.

"No. In the Starter Zone your main focus is on the physical abilities of a fae. In the Traveler's Zone, you will level from 20 to 40.

During this time, you will focus on learning new magical abilities. Oh, you will continue leveling your strength and agility along with intellect and spirit. But you will not learn any new physical abilities until you train in the following Zone.

I frown. I guess that means I'll be losing him, too.

"Okay. But you said I need to choose my trainer? Why? Do they teach different things? Do I need to specialize?" I think back to my conversation with Darlene on the day I was inscribed. "I thought fae were the one race that could learn all types of spells and physical abilities."

"We are," Tanyl replies, pausing on the garden path. "But the Traveler's Zone is divided into two factions. Players generally choose one or the other to support. They build amenity with the quests they perform for their chosen faction until they reach exalted level. By completing those quests, they lose amenity with the other side until they reach the hated status."

"Being 'hated' means the NPCs will attack on sight, right?"

"Very succinctly put. Being attacked without engaging the fight first is not something you encountered in the Starter Zone. Well, except for your training. Which is why our time together was so important. Preparation is everything."

"What types of quests will I be doing for the factions?"

"Getting materials, fighting off invaders, participating in battles, eventually leading war parties if you prove talented enough."

"And there's one trainer in each area," I say, mostly to myself. I look up at him. "How do I choose? Which faction is better?"

"Do you want the backstory—which side fights for what purpose. What each one believes. Who drew first blood?"

"No." I shake my head. "I'm sure the narrative is interesting. The hydrologists are trying to entertain us after all. But that story isn't real. They invented it. Someone wrote it just like people used to write stories for movies in my old world."

"Ah, but there's a difference here. The NPCs don't know its fiction. It's their lives. They believe the story line as much as you believe the history of your own world. The conflicts run deep—

"And then?" I interrupt.

"And then what?"

"They die, right? Players rez, but those NPCs die during the battles."

He frowns. "Yes, it is a continuing storyline. There are similar quests for all players, but it is never exactly the same. The story evolves based on the choices you make. The world evolves."

"So when Alby and L.G. are ready to go through the quests, it won't be the same. Things I choose to do, things other players do, will alter the future quest lines."

"Correct."

Players are free to choose. But those choices include consequences. If they didn't have consequences, it wouldn't be true freedom.

"We effect the world, but the world doesn't affect us. Because we're players. Immortals." I shake my head. "No matter what scrape we get into, we always get out of it. This isn't right."

"What isn't?"

"The Starter Zone quests were simple. Rescuing a cat from a tree to make a little girl happy. Getting a book for someone off a high shelf. Learning basic skills like cooking or mining. Picking flowers."

"What do you mean, child?"

"You just said that if I was talented enough I could lead war parties. Killing people on the other side. Or failing the quest and having the NPCs that I lead die. Right?"

"Yes."

"And if the quest fails, picking it up again, leading more NPCs into a slightly different battle… On and on it goes. It doesn't matter who's right and who's wrong because the NPCs all end up with the short end of the stick. And no one cares. Because it's the story."

"Correct. No one cares."

"I care."

Tanyl stares like he's trying to read my mind. "This is a strange sentiment for a person who spent every night over the last few months fighting random creatures in the Training Room."

I stare at him. "You know about that?"

"Yes, I do."

"I thought I was being quiet." I take a deep breath, and exhale slowly. "I'm not naive. I know that some creatures in the Traveler's Zone will attack me on sight. Mindless beings created by the Hydrologists without sentience. Some NPCs may attack as well, although I hope I can avoid that."

"Why?" he pushes.

"I want to explore the world. I want to learn, to level up, to do exciting things. I want to earn gold and get new gear. I don't want to ferment war. To kill people that won't come back to life. To tear apart families for the sake of a fictional story."

"Most players would say that the NPCs are not real people. That they don't have real families."

"I'm not like most players. I hope to heaven I never will be." My voice breaks. "I've killed people in the real world. People that deserved to die. People who were trying to hurt me. To hurt Alby. I don't want to kill people here for ..." I pause. "For fun. For entertainment."

"I believe you. There is a third choice. A harder way forward."

"I don't mind if it's harder. My dad used to say nothing worth doing is ever easy."

He nods and waves his hand at me.

*Quest Offered: Just Because There's No Path Doesn't Mean You're Lost.*

*Difficulty May Vary. Reward: Unknown. Yes or No?*

"Yes." I say.

"Follow me." With that he turns and walks through the portal. I hurry to catch up. We materialize back at the border of the Starter Zone.

"Go through the barrier. Find your own way forward." His voice is gruff, but a bit of moisture sparkles in the corner of his eye.

"Tanyl..." I hesitate, not sure what to say. Not sure if I should acknowledge his show of emotion. "Thank you."

He reaches over and claps me on the shoulder. "I feel like I should give you some wise advice. Something to speed you along your journey. But this isn't goodbye. I'm still here if you need me."

"I can still visit the Training Room if I can't sleep?"

"Of course, but I hope you won't need to." He clears his throat. "This isn't an ending,

Cami. It's a beginning. Your life can be anything you want it to be. Make it worthwhile."

# Chapter Thirteen

*W*arning! You are approaching the barrier between the Traveler's Zone and the Starter Zone. Review: Yes/No?

"Yes."

*In the Traveler's Zone not every creature or NPC is friendly. New areas of the world are apt to have more unfriendly encounters until a player builds amity. Even with the best intentions, though, there are some creatures that will attack players on sight. There is no opportunity to build amity. Learning to spot the intent of an NPC or creature from a distance is essential for survival. Review: Yes/No?*

It's not exactly new information, but a good review. The last time I encountered this explanation was at the border between the Starter Zone and the Open World Raid of the Spider Queen's cave, and that did not end well. In fact, I died and it took several hours for me to rez. "Yes."

*Friendly NPCs and creatures will appear with a light-green aura. Neutral NPCs with whom a player can develop amity also will have a light-green aura. Warning: Players can also lose amity with this type of NPC through a variety of actions. Neutral creatures have a yellow aura and will not attack a player unless attacked first. Neutral NPCs who have a yellow aura will not attack a player unless attacked first. There is a possibility to build amity with these NPCs. Players can lose amity if they attack the NPCs. Eventually a player will lose enough amity that the NPCs of that area will become hostile. Hostile creatures and NPCs will have a red aura. These will attack a player on sight.*

The two factions that Tanyl mentioned earlier. Suddenly I wish I had let him give me more information. At least their names. But it's too late now. He left, off to train new students no doubt, and I don't want to go back. It would be too much like dragging my feet.

I step through the barrier. At first it does not look different. The same grass, flowers, and bushes dot the countryside. Tree branches cut into a clear blue sky. A few minutes walking and the foothills start rising.

Soon they tower above me, giving way to high, slanting walls of stone with a single pass leading through them.

The pass widens, narrows, and widens again. I climb steadily upwards. I could switch to **Flight Form**, but I don't want to hurry through the area. I walk slowly, looking for anything new. Nothing sparkles to draw my attention. No new flowers. No new herbs. Nothing so far to gather for Alby and L.G.

The air is cooler here, and there is the damp smell of moss. I don't know how far I have traveled, but I realize that the Hydrologists designed the landscape in this way. To funnel players in a specific direction after they leave the Starter Zone.

There's a break in the wall and from the view I realize just how high I have climbed. Far below a cataract plunges hundreds of feet and vanishes from sight behind a rocky spur. Much farther below, a large stream meanders across a plain and winds its way through a dark forest. There are broken towers upon the plain. The remains of a battle, or perhaps several battles, are scattered about the landscape.

I continue walking. The path slopes downward and I catch sight of a man-made object in the distance. I hurry forward. It is a stone with words and symbols carved in English. It sits right at the edge of a road traveling east to west.

The town of Jenan lies 5 miles east and the town of Reme lies 5 miles west.

Which to choose? I need more information.

I activate the game interface map by focusing on the quest title, **Just Because There's No Path Doesn't Mean You're Lost**. A glowing golden line, the game's answer to a GPS, appears on the earth and heads south into the forest. Off in the distance I see a straight glowing neon-blue line shoot up toward the sky.

Of course my destination doesn't have a handy-dandy road to follow. That's just peachy.

On the other hand, there are bound to be more chances to pick flowers and herbs in the forest. All clouds have silver linings if you just look for them, as the expression goes.

That wasn't one of my dad's sayings, though. He was a bit more realistic about life. Some things that happen are just plain bad.

But this trek starts providing positive results almost immediately. A few feet from the road I spot a tell-tale glimmer and find a plant with small, bell-like flowers. I pick it immediately and receive new information from the AI.

*Congratulations! You have reached a new level of the Herbalism Skill. Current gathering level: Skilled 10. Herbalism allows you to find and harvest herbs and plants scattered throughout the realm. It is a primary profession linked with the skills of alchemy and cooking, although herbs may be useful in other professions as well.*

*Congratulations! Your knowledge is increasing. You have unlocked lore on Lilly of the Valley. Review: Yes/No?*

"Yes."

*Lilies of the Valley are classified as among the vast collection of flowers and herbs used for alchemy. Known for their strong fragrance, they are generally located in valleys or along coastlines. The flowers can be combined with other materials when using the alchemy skill.*

*Alchemy will imbue the item with additional benefits. No known use in cooking. Warning: Poisonous if ingested raw.*

The new skill level is encouraging. Everyone starts at Beginner 1 and then moves up in the rankings. Fae have an innate ability to find useful herbs and plants with greater ease than other races. Even though we obsessively "herb," as my sister calls the act of picking the flowers and plants, Alby, L.G., and I have been sitting at Skilled 9 for a very long time.

I'm glad that I won't be returning home empty-handed. I pick as many as I can find and I'm rewarded with a few seeds for my trouble. We should be able to grow some of these when we plant a garden.

I've wandered a bit, but I'm not worried. The in-game GPS adjusts to my ramblings and continuously recalculates the quickest way to my destination. There really is no way to get lost as long as I use the tools provided by the Hydrologists.

The AI is being helpful again. As I focus on trees, bushes, and even grass it provides information. Most of it is general. Any type of tree when cut will provide logs, for instance.

But some types of trees have other benefits for alchemy, woodworking, and weapon smithing. I figure there will be time to gather items after I find my trainer, though, and don't go into a frenzy of collecting items.

There is a calmness in this place I find refreshing. I have not seen any other players or NPCs. I have not seen any creatures larger than chittering squirrels. Which is why the explosion comes as a total surprise. There is no flash or blast or any other sign of its cause, but I both feel and hear the boom.

Two explosions in two days. In vastly different areas of the realms. What are the chances of that?

Above the tree line floats an airship close to three hundred feet long with a slightly rounded wooden hull. Ropes attach the lower portion of the ship to an inflated balloon-like aspect, bright white in color with an identification symbol, a red bird with white-tipped feathers extended in flight, inside a round yellow circle in the center of the canvas. The deck is manned with archers and swordsmen. There are two sets of fore and aft catapults.

What I don't see are cannons or any other type of a gun large enough to account for the sound of the explosion.

The ship pivots in the air, coming around to point directly at what looks like an oncoming flock of five large birds. Or creatures. They are too big and too strange looking to be birds. They drift closer, flapping their wings.

A moment passes before I realize that they are not creatures either. They are some sort of gliders. A person hangs below each set of the feathered wings, which flap and move with mechanical precision in a sky washed out by the morning sun.

The archers nock their arrows and aim at the flock.

The gliders draw in their wings and dive toward the deck, covering the distance in a few heartbeats. Most of the arrows fly uselessly past the attack force and fall like black rain from the sky. The archers aimed and released the volley too late.

The forward catapult releases a torrent of small rocks at the lead glider. It is a scatter-shot approach that proves effective. There are so many missiles that it is impossible to dodge them all.

But at the moment the stones strike, the other four let loose with fireballs. Spheres of crackling flame spring from their hands, glowing faintly at first and then with increasing brightness. The balls of fire shoot from their hands like bullets from a gun and fly toward the ship, exploding. Pieces bounce off the hull and fall to the ground, throwing hissing, burning globs of magic-fueled fire in all directions, setting everything they touch aflame.

They're mages, I realize. Humans who specialized in magic and chose to follow the path of fire, ice, and other forms of destruction. I try to prompt the AI to provide information, but the figures are too far away. The AI remains quiet. From this distance I can't even tell if they are Players or NPCs.

Soldiers onboard the ship scream in pain but hold their positions. The catapult in the stern lines up with another one of the attackers and let loose a second volley of stones. The shot goes wide of the mark and a waterfall of stones roar down only a few yards away from where I stand, watching the battle.

I cannot believe how loud the impact of the stones sound as they hit the upper branches of the trees. The mages regroup and sling another round of fireballs.

The ropes catch fire, the flames speeding up toward the balloon. For a brief moment I wonder what keeps the vehicle aloft. Is it hot air or some type of gas? Then a horrible sound and a blinding light answers my question.

The explosion tears through the ship in a lacework of fire. Shards and splinters of wood from the hull fly outward, knocking the gliders out of the air. The bulk of the craft crashes against the tops of the trees, causing the towering pines and oaks to snap like twigs as it continues its path downward.

The ground shudders with the impact. I throw my arm in front of my face to shield my eyes, my heart thundering somewhere in the vicinity of my throat. The force manages to knock me off of my feet and my head cracks violently against the ground.

The forest has transformed to flame and smoke. Burning branches snap and fall in showers of sparks. I climb to my feet and back away without thinking, trying to put some distance between myself and the flames. My throat and nose burn from the smoke. But then I hear a voice. I hear screams. Someone is inside that flaming wreckage. Someone needs help.

# Chapter Fourteen

I run forward. The screams grow louder. I cast **Slow Heal** on myself more as a precaution than anything else and keep moving. The heat is horrible. Suddenly from out of the haze and smoke the shape of a mound of rubble appears. A young man, perhaps in his late twenties, with red hair, a beard, and pointed ears is pinned beneath a large piece of timber. His eyes are shut and his face contorts in agony. The earth next to him changes into scarlet mud.

I cast **Slow Heal** on him immediately.

*Finn O'lalen, Ambassador of the Woedboran*

*Alignment: Neutral*

*Level 40.*

An NPC, then, and not a player, although I haven't heard the term Woedboran before. The AI's voice is somewhat reassuring as it identifies him, particularly the fact that he's neutral. But the interface would be more helpful if it told me the extent of his injuries. I can't see any type of aura glow among the flames and the smoke to know if the light is steady or flickering heavily.

I pull a medium-sized health potion from my bags. His eyes snap open at my approach and narrow in distrust.

"I'm here to help." I'm at a loss for words but plunge forward regardless. "I have a health potion." I hold it toward him.

A smile tugs at his lips despite his obvious pain. "I can't reach it. You'll have to help me a bit more."

Although his voice is filled with stress and pain, his accent comes through.

"You're British?" I ask as I kneel next to him.

"I don't know what that is, darlin'. Name's Finn O'lalen of the Woedboran." I hold the bottle to his lips and he drinks. "Ah, that helps. Thank you."

Right. NPCs in this realm don't know about any world except this one. References like British or American won't mean anything to them. I will have to shift my frame of reference when speaking.

I also notice that he didn't mention he's an ambassador. Interesting that the AI tells me more than he seems to want me to know. I file that away for later analysis while I cast **Slow Heal** on him again.

*Amity with the Woedboran increased by 100. Alignment: Neutral.*

"You're welcome," I say automatically. "I'm Cami. One of the fae." The fire flares near us as another explosion rocks the remainder of the ship. "I'm going to try lifting this timber off you. Do you think that you can try, I don't know, wriggling out of there?"

"I bloody will if you can shift this!"

I cast **Slow Heal** on both of us as the embers fall, searing our exposed skin. Fortunately my gear seems, if not fire-proof, at least fire resistant. I wrap my fingers around the wooden beam and heave. It is heavier than anything I could have lifted as a human, but my fae body is far stronger. All of those level boosts to my strength stats are paying off.

Finn groans as the timber rises. He pushes down on the ground with his arms, propelling his body backward. As soon as he is clear, I drop the timber and rush to his side.

"Hold on to me." I pull him to his feet. Well over seven feet tall, he matches me in height. I half-carry him, using the in-game GPS once again to guide my steps. The line is still set to lead me to my trainer. It's a good thing that I have that ability, because the thick smoke makes it difficult to navigate. I want to cough but know if I start I won't be able to stop until I can take a clear breath of air.

The smoke, the sunlight muted by the huge cloud of dust, the noise of the ship settling and trees groaning, almost overwhelms me. My throat and nose are burning even with the **Slow Heal** buff. Each breath sends a sharp pain through my chest. When we emerge from the smoke and hit the clean air, I manage to guide Finn a bit farther until I'm certain we are upwind from the smoke. We take cover behind a clump of bushes, although anyone with a set of ears could find us from the coughing.

The smell of burning timbers, gas, and scorched bodies lingers in my nose. It coats the inside of my lungs. I feel like I can't cough enough to clear them. It's the smell of war and hatred.

I pull two more healing potions from my bags. They are medium-sized potions, faster-working than the **Slow Heal** spell. Sort of a one-shot health boost while **Slow Heal** works over time to return health. I hand one to Finn and gulp the other.

The liquid tastes sweet and immediately calms my coughing. Tingling chills run through my body and the burns go numb for a moment as my skin starts to heal. I follow up the potion with another cast of **Slow Heal** for both of us. That's all I can do for now. My mana level is about two thirds depleted and I want to hold some in reserve, just in case.

"Thank you …"

"Glad I could help," I say. I turn my attention back toward the burning husk of the ship. "I can't hear any other cries. Any other survivors." I turn back to face him. "I'm sorry."

He nods, closing his eyes for a moment, the grief etched on his features. "Fire is a horrible way to die." He opens his eyes, focusing on my own. "Had it not been for your actions, I surely would have shared their fate."

"I just wish I could do more."

"Are you all right?" he asks. He reaches out to gently touch the side of my face. "You are burned."

"I'm healing." I'm so startled by his action that I don't move. I stare at his face, mere inches from my own. I realize that I haven't been this physically close to a stranger in years. Well, not really years. But it's been a few months. When I helped Michael escape from the hospital after we both had been captured by the soldiers, I had helped him walk because his ribs were broken.

So, my brain insists, I haven't been this close to any strangers in years except severely injured men. My rules about maintaining distance to protect myself from potential harm are still in place. Sort of.

Somehow this sounds like a cop-out.

"It's part of my magic. The healing spell," I explain.

"It's good magic."

"It's not as strong as I'd like, but I'm going to my trainer to learn more. To get stronger."

Oh lord, stop babbling. He doesn't need to know this. Why am I still talking?

"I'm sure you will excel—"

I hold up a hand to halt Finn's words. Coughs and raspy voices fill the air, not too far from our position. They have a different accent than Finn. It sounds American to my ears.

"Your people?" I move close to him, whispering in his ear.

He shakes his head and mouths a single word. "Pirates."

# Chapter Fifteen

"**C**an you move on your own?"
He nods.
"I'll lead them away. Do you have somewhere safe to go? Where they can fully treat your wounds?"

"Yes. We're not too far from the borders of my land. Once I'm there the magic of my people will sustain me until I reach a healer." He reaches out and grabs my arm as I turn to leave. "Meet me in the GreenWood when you can. I would like to thank you properly for saving my life."

*Quest Offered: **This Took an Unexpected Turn**.*

*Difficulty May Vary. Reward: Unknown. Yes or No?*

"Yes," I say, both to him and to the A.I. I pull away and use **Transform** to shift into panther form.

The shocked look on Finn's face is priceless. "You're certainly full of surprises."

He must not have met a fae before. I grin and cast **Shadowform,** fading from view.

"Full of surprises …" He turns and limps away from the voices, holding on to the trees for support. The leaves rustle with his passage.

In panther form my eyes work better than normal. I hear noises from farther away than humanly possible. Normally my sense of smell also works overtime, but in this instance the smoke and ash block anything else from coming through.

I stalk forward through the brush, avoiding the burning embers. The flames have died down somewhat. The forest is fresh and green with no dry brush for the fire to consume. Good thing, or the destruction might continue unchecked.

I move slowly through the bushes. Shadowform may make me invisible, but it does not cover up the rustle of the leaves and grass that brush against my body. I want to get to the other side of the pirates and then make enough noise to draw them in that direction. Away from Finn.

I can distinguish two, no three, separate voices growling conspiratorially among themselves. Furious that their magical fire spread to the balloon and ignited the gas. Each one blaming the other.

"There's no profit here," one man complains. "No prey. No pay."

"We didn't do this for the loot on board the ship. You know that," another voice, a female, snaps. "We need to find the Ambassador's body. Proof of death."

"In this mess? Are ye kidding?" Exasperation fills the third person's voice.

"Yes, in this mess! Or don't ye want to get paid?" Her voice drips with sarcasm. "So show a leg."

I'm within view now, peering through a screen of leaves. Under their dark robes the three mages are dressed in colorful tunics full of knotted tassels and colorful, geometric patches. The men wear black trousers and the woman a black skirt. More importantly, their auras are bright red, which means they will attack on sight.

I focus on the woman, who seems to be in charge, and the AI chimes in with new information.

*Cheville Jambe*
*Boatswain of The Deadlights*

*Alignment: Hated*

*Level 30*

The men are identified as level 20 crewmen. They are both named Murry.

That must be confusing as all get out for the NPCs. Unless all crewmen are named Murry. Which would show a lack of imagination on the part of the Hydrologists. Or an in-joke I just don't get.

"Blimey, ye're just on fire today—literally," Murry One says.

The woman looks down at her leg, screams and starts rolling on the ground to extinguish the flames. "Help me!"

"What profit is there for me in that? Besides, it's out now." Murry Two grins, showing front teeth capped in gold.

"That leg looks painful," Murry One chimes in. "Raw and charred."

"How embarrassing for a fire mage to catch fire herself."

"And losing two crewmen to boot. Imagine what the captain will say."

"Scupper that!" Cheville pops open a health potion and takes a deep gulp. The skin on her leg heals instantly. "Shut yer yaps, both of you, or you'll rue the day yer mothers ever spawned you!"

"Hold up!" Murry Two raises his hand. "I hear something. That way." He points in the direction Finn headed.

Drat!

With no more time to plan or position myself, I dash away from the pirates, making as much noise as possible. "This way, Ambassador!" I cry out, trying to mimic an English accent. It wouldn't fool anyone under normal circumstances, but I'm hoping Cheville and the two Murrys will take the bait.

Their shouts echo behind me and they run in my direction, their boots catching on roots and stones that my panther feet flow gracefully over. I can't move as fast in **Shadowform** but I don't want them to spot me. If the pirates catch a glimpse, they will realize that I'm not a Woedboran. I'm not dressed in the livery of the soldiers on board the ship. In other words, they won't be able to collect a bounty on me.

Although the pirates come up in the AI as a hated status, I'm not sure why. Are they just the standard in-game enemy? NPCs players are meant to encounter and kill over and over again? Is that why the two men are both named Murry?

I could turn about and fight with them, but I don't want to kill any sentient NPCs if I can avoid it. They don't respawn after dying like the NPC monsters created for the dungeons and raids or the non-sentient animals in forest. They are not like the constructs I fight in the Training Room, spawned for a particular purpose. Regular NPCs have a life. Experience the world. They grow from childhood to adulthood. They have families.

Are there family and friends who would miss Cheville and the two Murrys if they die? I simply don't know. So I run rather than engaging them in battle and lead them away from Finn.

Why are they killing other NPCs, though? Some Hydrologist designed them to be this way. Programed them with this back story so they would hate Players, I guess. And hate Woedboran. Maybe they hate anyone who isn't a pirate.

If they are self-aware, they would realize their situation. Hating everyone who isn't exactly like them is a horrible way to live.

Fortunately, all three chase me. They shout back and forth to each other in excitement. No doubt they anticipate the bounty price their quarry will bring.

After ten minutes, I pick a high tree and begin to climb. By the time they reach the base, I'm twenty feet up. I'm still basically invisible in **Shadowform,** as long as they don't hear me. I hope the pounding of my heart isn't loud enough to draw attention.

I also hope that I can keep from coughing. Just the thought of it makes me uncomfortable. I feel the need to at least clear my throat, but I fight it.

"Lost them again. The Captain will have a field day with ye."

Her face gleams hot with rage. "Hold your tongue and your whinin' for them that's at your beck and call, because I ain't."

"Ye may be soon. Cap'n don't hold with failure. Time for a demotion I think. And I'll be sure to tell him who's fault this is. Who lost her temper and shot at the gas-filled bag rather than the hull!"

"Avast!" Cheville cries. Her eyes widen in horror as she looks over the crewman's shoulder.

Murry One spins to face the danger behind him and puts the true menace at his back. Cheville pulls a dagger out from a sheath on her hip and slips it into his spine.

"By all that's great and good," Murry Two breaths. "Why would ye do that?" His voice is whiny. "He weren't all that bad."

Cheville whirls toward him, not watching the body fall to the earth. "The Woedboran's could just as easily have killed every one of ye. Make your choice. Liar or corpse."

Murry Two glances down at his fallen brethren. "I didn't see nothing." The whine has gone out of his voice. Now he sounds resigned.

Cheville turns a wary eye on him. "Cross me and I'll watch you dance the yardarm jig." She looks off in the distance. "Get on before the border patrols arrive. We've a short time now."

With a last glance at his fallen comrade, Murry Two heads off into the woods.

Cheville stands there, her legs spread, speaking to the sky. "All right Woedboran! You've had your little victory! Enjoy it! Upon my life none of you shall escape my vengeance. I'll fly your bloody head as my banner!"

She stalks off into the woods, following Murry Two. I wait for several minutes. They might have only been pretending to leave while they actually crept back toward the area, waiting for me to make a mistake.

At last when I decide it is safe to leave the tree and continue on the quest line toward my trainer, I notice Murry One's life signs. The red aura flickers with the last moments of his life.

Cheville didn't quite kill him. Almost without thinking I shift back to fae form and cast **Slow Heal**. The flickering slows as his aura grows stronger. He lifts his head, squinting at me, not certain what has happened. His blue eyes widen and he starts in surprise when he realizes who has healed him.

I drop a health potion near his hand and shift to **Flightform** before he can recover and attack. Leaping into the air, I pump my wings, wheeling once to see if he drinks it. He does and for a moment it looks like his aura shifts from hated red to neutral yellow. But I can't be sure, and my flight has taken me too far away for the AI to give me any information.

But the thought nags at me. The AI has said repeatedly that there's no way to build amity with NPCs who have red auras. So how could anything I do change that? Is it really a hard-and-fast rule that cannot be altered?

Or have I done something that the game did not expect? Sideways thinking that breaks the rules? And how can I find out?

Still, it would be nice to think that Murry One recognizes a helping hand when he sees one. That my actions may have changed his mind just a little bit about outsiders.

# Chapter Sixteen

I pick up the trail to my trainer's home and fly for more than thirty minutes before my final destination appears. I fight the temptation to fly overhead and scout the area before landing. Somehow it seems rude to spy. I want to start off on a good foot.

I land and shift back to my usual fae form. In a few minutes I come upon a small clearing. The GPS line fades away as I step onto the green lawn ringed by oak and apple trees. At the edge of the grove, between two trees just coming into blossom, stands a little A-Frame house of wattle and daub. It is a very primitive affair and not what I expect.

I scan the area, looking for a large enough tree in the grove that could hold a house. Although the trees are old growth, they are not large enough to carve out for a residence. So the little house in the center of the grove must be where my trainer lives.

A fire burns in a pit in front of the little house with a cauldron sitting on an improvised stand above the flames. Steam rises and drifts on the currents of air, bringing delicious scents.

Stirring the cauldron is a middle-aged fae woman dressed in a green robe of some fine and precious fabric. Her shirt is covered at the wrists and neck with intricate pin-tucks and lacy edges, buttoned with a row of minute pearl buttons. The woman's appearance contrasts with the rustic nature of the dwelling. Her skin is a golden brown and gleams in the light. A cloud of hair as silver as my own is crowned with a circlet of green fronds, ivy and ferns, and studded with white roses and starry leaves.

*Fae Trainer: Level: 40. Alignment: Neutral*

"Hold, girl!" comes a voice, low-pitched and throaty, so forceful that I stop in my tracks. "What wicked and wild wind blows you into my glen?"

"My Starter Zone trainer, Tanyl Xillamin, gave me a quest to find my next trainer. The quest GPS line led here."

"Did he now? And a quest line you say?" The woman stares at me, her head twisting first one way and then the other, as a bird might examine its prey before pouncing. Finally she said, "Good! Good! What is your name, girl?"

"Cami."

*Quest Complete! Meet Your Trainer. Reward: **Fae Fire**. Experience gained.*

*Congratulations player! You have learned the spell: **Fae Fire**.*

*Cast Time: 1 Second*

*Cool Down: None*

*Cost: 10 Mana*

*Damages 10 percent of player's spell power to a single target.*

Interesting. **Fae Fire** does the same amount of damage as **Claw**, which is the first offensive melee ability I learned from Tanyl. But this uses mana rather than energy. And magic spells are ranged. I can attack from a distance rather than having to be close enough to my target to rake my claws into it and still have full amount of energy when I use a melee ability.

A Fae's stats are all equal, which makes us unique among the player classes. We receive 1% of Agility, Strength, Intellect, and Spirit per level. Other classes specialize, focusing on Agility and Strength for Warriors and Thieves or Intellect and Spirit for Casters. As Darlene said months ago during our initial introduction to the Realms, a Warrior will never be able to cast a spell and a Mage will never be able to effectively wield a sword.

But the Fae class can do it all.

My base Spell Power is 20, but the gear I wear boosts my stats. And I have been extraordinarily lucky in that regard. Because of a glitch, I was able to loot two pieces of gear from a Level 50 Open World Raid Zone, the Helm of Athene and the Harness of Athene. These pieces, incorporated with my other level 20 gear and weapons, increase my Agility to 115 and my Intellect to 115.

Of course my stats are still equal. A little bit of irony by the hydrologists. Or is something else at work?

Basically I have a 50 point boost over most other level 20s in both stats. Which really doesn't sound like a lot until you do the math, which is not something I enjoy. Since Attack Power is equal to the amount of Agility and Spell Power is equal to Intellect, I am overpowered for the enemies I will face in the Traveler's Zone. I kept one-shotting level 20 constructs in Tanyl's training room until I removed the constraints and had it spawn creatures that had a similar gear score.

Ganking things, a term I learned from Kickerz that means 'running around and killing things less powerful than you', is not fun. Facing down my enemy. Winning or losing based on my own merits. This is fun.

"Ah, yes. You're late."

I sigh. What is this obsession NPCs have with non-existent time-tables? "I didn't know I had an appointment."

"You didn't." She grins. "My brother suggested I say that to you."

"Your brother." I take a second look at her face. Her features do seem familiar. "Tanyl is your brother."

"Of course. He thought you would figure it out sooner or later but wanted to have some fun before you realized. He has a dry sense of humor." She bows with a flourish. "Myke Xillamin at your service."

I smile. "It's a relief—"

"What?" She interrupts, a frown creasing her forehead. "You mean what trees do in the spring?"

"What?"

"Re-leaf."

"I don't understand."

"Oh dear. I'm doing it again. Let me try words that make that sentence make more sense." She opens her mouth for a moment, and then presses her lips together without making a sound, and shrugs. "I don't have any other words. We'll have to make due with these."

"What?" I've lost the thread of this conversation somehow.

"Make due. You know, like if your parents or grandparents were going through hard times and didn't have enough money. They would make due. And it probably wasn't very tasty. Due never is. But it's filling," Myke says, pointing at me for emphasis. "And that's the most important part about due. That it's filling. Remember that."

"Is that what's cooking in your pot over the fire?" I ask.

"Oh no." She walks over to the kettle. "Would you like a taste? It's vegetable cheese soup. One of my favorites." She picks up a mug from a stack near the fire and ladles out a serving.

"Thank you." The scent of the food makes my stomach rumble with hunger. I take a deep breath, let it out, then accept the offered mug. "It smells absolutely wonderful!"

"It should. It's the farthest thing from due I can think of. Or is it?" A frown creases her forehead. "Can food be measured in distance?"

"I don't think so." I pause before taking a sip. This woman is so strange. Is there a chance she's given me poison?

Myke scoops out a serving for herself and takes a drink. "Carethul. It's thot." She waves her hand in front of her open mouth. "Don't thurn yorth tung."

I piece together what she says and then reflexively cast **Slow Heal** on her. I blow away some of the steam from my own mug, hoping that she mistakes the reason for my hesitation. But no such luck.

"Thank you for the heal. Are you worried the soup is poisoned?" She studies me intently.

"It did occur to me." I blink. "I've had some experiences with witches in the game during the All Hallows event."

"And you think I'm one? Oh my dear. Didn't Tanyl teach you anything?"

"No. Well, yes, he did." I stutter. "But not about fae magic."

"He didn't teach you **Slow Heal**? Goodness. That's unexpected. You learned it on your own?"

"Yes. Well. No." I'm fumbling over my words and rack my mind for the proper way to answer. "Tanyl taught me about **Slow Heal**. I didn't think …"

"I'm starting to see that. And I assume he taught you about **Cleanse**. Although I shouldn't assume. You know what they say about people who assume?"

"No." I'm sticking with one-word answers. It might be less embarrassing. I can't believe I forgot about **Cleanse**, which removes most poison, disease, and magical effects. I take a sip and immediately cast **Slow Heal** on myself to soothe my burnt lips and tongue. The soup is too hot to drink but tastes marvelous. A rich and hearty broth with the unexpected sharp flavor of cheddar cheese bits.

"It makes an '***' out of 'u' and 'me'." She tilts her head. "That sounded funny. I mean, it's supposed to because it's a joke, but it sounded strange."

"It's the curse blocker."

"Really? But it's part of the freaking word. And it's not even a curse. It's an animal. Really? I can say 'donkey' but not '***'? It's getting so bad you have to substitute words that sound naughty just so you can be understood." She shakes a fist at the sky. "Stop messing with my words, you mother forklifts!"

"Maybe I should come back later." I hold out the mug to her, ready to back away. Perhaps I can find one of the other trainers to continue my education.

"Don't be silly. I rail at the Hydrologists all of the time. I think they're used to the abuse by now. Or they're just not listening." She shrugs with one shoulder. "One or the other."

"Okay." I draw out the word. Obviously Myke knows about the Hydrologists. Perhaps it makes sense that trainers would know more about players and their past lives. Or perhaps Tanyl told her.

"But now back to fae magic. You have questions and I have answers, girl. Shall we see if they match?"

# Chapter Seventeen

"I do have questions." I take another cautious sip of soup, glad that it's cool enough now to drink without fear of burning my mouth. The shredded cheese is thicker at the bottom of the cup. I wish I had a spoon to scoop it all up.

Myke's shoulders sag in evident disappointment. "Apparently you are not good at this game. That's not even remotely a question. That's why people are ill-informed. You've got to ask questions."

"True. Okay. What's the difference between the magic of a witch, mage, wizard, and fae?" I might as well ask her a question that's been bothering me ever since I saw the pirate mages. I hadn't seen NPCs with that type of magic before.

"Ah. My answer was going to be 'little pink house.' But that doesn't fit, does it?"

I find myself smiling. "No. It doesn't."

"Well, if I were you, I would include all the types of magic workers in my question. You forgot clerics and enchanters. Of course, that would be strange. If I were you." Myke pauses and tilts her head. "Who would you be? That's an important question to be sure. And you've got to ask questions. You have to ask to find out. That's why people lose all direction. If you don't ask questions—"

"Can you include clerics and enchantresses in your answer?" I interrupt. It's rude, but I don't want her going off on another tangent. I'm having trouble following the current conversation on magic. If we start adding other topics I won't be able to keep up.

"Yes. Of course." She beams at me. "That was easy. Give me another."

I sigh and consider for a moment on how to phrase my question. "What is the difference between the types of magic workers in this realm?"

"Ah. That is a good question and will take more than a few words. Come inside. Bring your soup."

I follow her through the doorway of the tiny A-Frame house of wattle and daub, expecting to see a small room, perhaps a kitchen, with a neatly made bed in the corner. The immense size, the sweeping grandeur, startles me. Marble floors, polished wood, velvet fabrics, frescoed ceilings, carved furniture.

"Is this house bigger on the inside than it is on the outside?"

"That's another question. I haven't even answered your first. Well, your second. I did answer the first. So yes. No, actually. Not really. But for purposes of this conversation. Yes."

I wonder if there are any plans for sale in MidWorld that would show me how to build a house like this? And how much those plans would cost?

"Come upstairs to the library. There are a few books I want you to read. You can take them home, but I want them back when you are finished. And mind you don't spill the soup. I don't want the books covered in cheese."

The staircase is steep, polished wood with a forest green runner. The wood smells of beeswax and the brass light fixtures gleam in the flickering lamplight. It is cooler in here by several degrees than the outside temperature.

The library. Oh my. I thought Tanyl's collection of books was impressive. Myke has hundreds of leather-bound volumes, regally decorated in gilt, lining the walls. There are two alcoves. Beneath each arched window a padded green-and-gold-velvet window seat provides a comfortable place to relax and read. A desk filled with paper-stuffed pigeonholes, colored in cut-glass bottles, and scattered pens and nibs, is positioned between the two main windows. There is a sweet smell of perfumed lamp oil.

"A library is not a luxury but one of the necessities of life," Myke comments. She heads to a green leather chair pulled up near one of the windows. "Ah. It's nice to get off my feet for awhile. Of course, I've never had the experience of being on anyone else's feet. That would be quite unusual to say the least." The frown line in her forehead deepens a bit. I imagine that she's thinking about walking around on someone else's feet. Figuring out how that could be possible.

I shake my head and walk over to the nearest alcove. Mindful of Myke's request about the cheese, I set my soup cup down on a coaster centered on a small marble-topped table.

Outside the windows the landscape is dark. In the gloom I make out large shapes, some familiar, some unfamiliar, and odd lights that twist and drift like they are on currents. Modern city skylines and masts of great sailing ships combine with strangely misshapen stones and cathedrals.

For a while I am caught in an eerie spell trying to make sense of what lies beyond the glass. Finally I step back and turn around. The little wattle-and-daub house I entered is in a forest. It's daylight. This interior, this view, should not exist. The fact the house is larger on the inside than the outside and has multiple exteriors opening into different realms is impossible on the surface.

Ah well. I accept the impossible daily in the Realms. Honestly, the Hydrologist's phrase "If you can imagine it, you can live it!" is really on display here. But who imagined this house? This view? Myke or the Hydrologists?

"Do the windows open? I don't see a latch."

"Oooh you are getting better at asking questions. That's a perfect interrogative." She takes a sip. "Mmmmm. Cheese."

"That's not an answer."

"Amazingly accurate."

"You know, for someone who said I should ask questions, you are not providing a lot of answers."

"I don't like providing answers to questions people should be able to figure out on their own."

I turn back toward the window and find a small brass crank. I reach out to touch it, to turn it, and Myke is immediately on her feet, her hand gripping my arm with firm pressure.

"Bravo. You figured it out. But let's not play with that right now."

Something is in front of the window. Some irregular shape which seems to be blocking much of the dim light. Whatever the darkness conceals, I don't want to let in to the room. I nod and she releases my arm. The shape becomes harder to see, as if it is fading away from the glass.

"There are basic answers to your question about magic. I'll provide those now. For more information you will need to do your own research." She takes her seat and waves at the books. "I won't spoon feed you the information. I will lend you the books you need."

"Deal." I hesitate before choosing a place to sit. No matter how comfortable the window seats appear, I don't want to be so close to the glass. I don't want to put my back toward the darkness.

Finally I choose the straight-backed chair by the desk.

"There are classes of magic. Rules established by the Hydrologists when they set up the Realms." She holds a finger up in the air. "Don't ask me about the reasoning behind these rules. They exist. I had nothing to do with creating them. So save the 'whys' for someone else."

My lips twitch into a smile. "No 'whys.' Got it."

"First of all. Every class has a trainer. These trainers teach players about their class. About their abilities. We are unique types of NPCs in the Game, having many of the same types of protections as players. Guess what that means."

"You have knowledge of the world outside the realms."

"And?"

I press my lips together for a moment before speaking. "You can't be killed? I mean, you can rez. Unlike the other NPCs."

"Correct. Otherwise there could be difficulties. Players might decide to kill us for some reason. Sport. Or to mess with players from other classes. And then there would be no one to provide training. So we're members of a 'protected class.'"

"Okay."

"And for this discussion we're excluding the limited types of NPCs spawned only for raids and dungeons. Those are a different kettle of fish all together."

I nod for her to continue.

"Unless it's a player or trainer, you will never see another fae in the game. You will see human and dwarf NPCs, but fae NPCs are forbidden." Myke spreads her hand out. "Tell me why."

"I thought you said no 'whys.'" I close my eyes for a moment, thinking. "Because certain magic is reserved for players and our magic is tied into our forms."

"Certain abilities. Not just magic."

"But I've seen NPC warriors …"

"No. You've seen NPC soldiers or guards. They do not have the same abilities as a warrior class player. Just like the fact that there can be NPCs who run around stealing stuff. Or highway men. Bandits. That type of sneaky person. But they won't have the same abilities as the thief class of players."

"I understand so far. Players are special. And the trainers who teach them are special, too."

"Other than the fae, which are a hybrid class specializing in both magic and melee, there are two types of player magic workers. Mages, who hone their abilities to do the most DPS possible …" She breaks off her sentence. "You know what DPS means, right?"

"Damage Per Second."

"Good. Where was I? Right. Wizards. They have a balance of damage and healing spells." She drains the last dregs of soup from her cup. "Lord, I love cheese."

I smile. "The other types you mention, the witches, enchanters, and clerics, are NPCs that correspond with the player classes."

"Yes. Witches practice natural magic, which is the closest to our own. Enchanters work destructive shadow magic. They don't work with the elements of fire and ice like mages, but they cast similar spells using shadow and darkness. And clerics heal. They really don't have the ability to do harm. Oh, I suppose they could hit someone with a shovel or other blunt instrument, but ..." She drifts off. "They're really pacifists. Not a lot of fire and brimstone in their natures."

"What about shifters?"

"Uhk. Don't get me started on those. They rarely leave Realm Two. And yes, they have their own magical quirks when changing form, but they lock into a specific class of mage, warrior, or thief."

"No wizards."

"Nope. They're undead, you see. So no healing spells."

"So there could be NPC vampires and werewolves in Ream Two, but they can't learn the skills reserved for players.

"Yep." She points at a stack of books on the desk. "You'll need to take those with you to read. Each volume covers the different player classes."

I pick up the tomes and slip them into my bag. "There's something bothering me. You said there can't be any NPC mages other than trainers, right?"

Myke nods. "Yep. There might be some in a dungeon or a raid. I don't have all of those fights memorized. But not out in the regular zones."

"But I've seen them."

"You have?"

"On my way here. I saw pirate mages bring down an airship."

# Chapter Eighteen

"Pirate mages?" Myke's voice cracks with amazement.

"Yes. In the forest between the Starter Zone and here. They used gliders to fly and shot fire balls at the Woedboran Ambassador's ship."

She looks me over from head to toe. "You don't look like you hit your head. Still when one babbles nonsense it's best to be sure." She lifts her hand. "How many fingers am I holding up? Wait before you answer that. Is the thumb a finger? I've never been sure. Ignoring the thumb, how many fingers am I holding up?"

I roll my eyes. "I'm fine. The AI identified them as a boatswain and crewmen. They called themselves fire mages."

"You heard them? From the ground."

"They were on the ground by that time. They crashed when the ship blew up."

"Who are they?"

"A woman named Cheville and two guys named Murry."

"I ... see." She raises her eyebrows. "Did you talk to them?"

"No. They had red auras."

"Continue." There is an edge to her command.

"Cheville stabbed one of the Murrys in the back and then left with the other Murry. I healed the injured Murry and left him a health potion. When I flew away, it looked like his aura changed color."

"What's that?" Myke asks and props a hand to her ear. "I'm certain I didn't hear you correctly. You healed him? Gave him a potion?"

"Yes."

"You do know that a red aura means he is your enemy? That he will try to kill you on sight?"

"Yes."

"Why heal him?"

"Because it was the right thing to do."

"Good answer. You might make a decent ..." She hesitates. "A decent Player one day."

"What do you mean?"

"Oh dear. I'm doing it again. Let me try words that make that make more sense." She scrunches up her mouth and then sighs. "Nope. We're going to have to stick with those words, I'm afraid. You'll just have to catch up."

"Why are they my enemy? I've never met them before this."

"Part of the story line." She tilts her head sharply to one side. Her eyes glitter. "You know about that I assume?"

I nod before she starts babbling about the word 'assume' again. "The conflict between Reme and Jenan?"

"Yes." A slow smile spreads over her face. "You didn't want to choose sides." It's a statement, not a question. "I know 'cause you're here and not in one of the two cities studying with less qualified trainers."

"I didn't want to kill NPCs who can't come back to life the way that I can."

She purses her lips and nods. "How interesting. May your choices always be so clear."

"Is the whole area divided."

"No. In fact the town where you link your Traveler's Zone portal, Neutram, is neutral. So are the Woedborans. And a lot of other small human and dwarf towns."

*Quest Offered: Journey to Neutram. Difficulty: Easy. Reward: Portal Access. Accept Yes/No?*

"Yes."

Myke tilts her head. "Do you want to know the history of the conflict?"

"Would it help?"

She shrugs. "Couldn't hurt. The red book on the desk. No, the one on the right. Dark red. Yes, you have it. That's the history of the region. The reasons behind the animosity. Why we're headed pell-mell toward a big battle."

I hold the book in my hand. "Can I stop it?"

"History?"

"No!" I take a deep breath. "The battle. The conflict. Can I stop it?"

"Good. I like that. You didn't ask if anyone could stop it or if we could stop it. You take responsibility, which is a good start. There's still room for improvement, though."

"I don't understand."

"You asked, dear, instead of stating 'I will stop it'. A bit disappointing." She sighs and rubs her hands together. "Still, you're young.

And it is a big task. And you're still learning the rules of the Game." She stops with a sigh. "Good lord! Could I make any more excuses? Well, yes. I could ..."

*Quest Offered: It Only Seems Impossible Until It's Done*

*Difficulty May Vary.*

*Reward: Unknown. Yes/No?*

"Yes."

Myke stands, tugging at her robe to straighten it. "Come on now, child. It's time for you to go home and improve your mind. The Professionum Scholae has half-day classes on the first day of each term. I believe school is about to dismiss for the day. You'll want to be there when your family returns."

I narrow my eyes. Tanyl must have told her about Alby and L.G. Is that common? Do the NPCs discuss all players this much?

Still, I'm glad Myke told me about the half-day. I want to be home when Alby and L.G. get there. I want to hear all about their day.

But I also realized that Myke has not answered my question. If regular, non-trainer NPCs can't be mages, then how did the pirates learn fire mage spells?

Why do I have the feeling she won't tell me the answer? There's something about this, something wrong, and I can't quite see what it is.

"Thank you," I say before activating my **Residence Stone**. "I appreciate your taking the time to train me. I appreciate the opportunity to learn more about fae magic."

*Congratulations! Amity with Myke Xillamin increased by 100. Alignment: Neutral.*

Simple politeness provides big dividends in this game.

"You look like you're waiting for something."

"It's just that your brother always says the same thing when we train. 'Learn something. Improve your mind.' I wondered if you had any parting words.

"Hmm. I don't know. Ohh! Yes I do." Myke clears her throat and stands a bit straighter. "Be careful when you're reading. Books don't have brains. So use your own."

I smile. "I like it."

"Thanks! I'll be sure to use it from here on out."

My **Residence Stone** glows brighter and brighter until the surroundings disappear. After about ten seconds the glow disappears and I arrive back at our Homestead in the area of the portal room. Before I even fully materialize both Alby and L.G. are jumping up and down in front of me, ready to tell me about their day.

"We made almost 1000 beginner health potions!" Alby says. "We cleared out a lot of low-level flowers from the bank."

"I got a clock for a quest reward. It's green." L.G. holds it up proudly. It's a wind-up alarm clock with two brass bells on the top.

"That will help us keep on time. Good job!"

He grins, flashing his white fangs.

"And we learned how to make 15 special food recipes. Oh, and I got a wooden shelf for a quest reward."

"Nice."

"I got a flower pot." He hands it to me. "It's for you. Because it's blue."

"Thanks L.G." I sweep him into a hug. "I want to hear all about your training and the school. Every minute. Oh, I picked some special flowers for you two. I even have a few seeds."

"Did you meet your new trainer?"

"You bet. And I can't wait to tell you all about Myke. She's Tanyl's sister."

"Really?"

"Yep."

Alby bites her lip, but the grin sneaks past.

"You're picturing Tanyl as a female, aren't you?"

"Mmhmm. Does she look like him?"

"A bit. No beard though." I pull out the books on magic from my bag. "She loaned me these."

"Cool! Can we read them too?"

"Yep. After dinner. Which you two will cook."

"Come on, L.G. The faster we finish, the faster we can read the books."

He looks up at me and grins. "Prepare to be impressed."

I smile. "I already am."

# Chapter Nineteen

After seeing L.G. and Alby off to school, I made the long flight to the city. I retraced a lot of my steps, but I did not stop to pick flowers or gather other materials. I wanted to make sure that I got here today and activated the portal.

*Quest Complete!* ***Journey to Neutram.*** *Reward: Portal Access. Review Yes/No?*

"Yes."

*Congratulations player! You have unlocked the portal to Neutram. Members of your party can now transport to Neutram, the central city in the Traveler's Zone. The portal is located in the center hub of the city in the Central Portal Room.*

*Review information on Neutram? Yes/No?*

"Yes."

*The center of commerce in The Traveler's Zone, Neutram serves as a sanctuary city. It provides a place where all races and alliances can co-exist peacefully. Run by Commander*

Platt, the government of Neutram allows all factions to interact within the city walls. PVP combat is forbidden.

City law must be followed at all times within the city limits. Failure to do so will result in legal consequences as determined by the city Commander. The only exceptions to this rule are in Guild Houses, where rules of behavior are set by the Guild Leaders.

Warning: **Residence Stones** can be activated only in certain areas of the city. These areas include the Inns, the Central Portal Room, and the Cathedral.

Warning: Because younger players can visit the city, the same rules and limitations apply to language and interactions in Neutram as they do in the Starter Zone. Since the area outside of the city contains higher-level enemies, players under the chronological age of 20 will not be allowed to leave the city limits.

Good to know. I'll have to plan a family trip here after I scope out the area.

There are so many players and NPCs filling the streets. People hawking and buying wares in outdoor shops. Street urchins chasing each other up and down between the stalls. Pack animals braying. The level of noise borders on being uncomfortable.

I activate my quest line GPS and trot through the crowds, catching snippets of conversations.

"Oh not again," one player says to another. "You really bought that **** from the vendor. Waste of money."

"Catch that raccoon!" Two young boys chase after the bewildered looking animal.

"No. I don't know where the clothing vendor is. Ask your guild."

"Part of me thinks this dungeon run is a really bad idea. Another part of me would really enjoy seeing you handed your *** again."

The line slants off down an alleyway. I'm glad to leave the crowds behind. I pass through the thieves training area filled with targets and dummies made out of sticks and straw. It's empty except for one female human player, who attacks the targets with gusto.

I don't recognize her until the interface pipes up.

*Wink Girl: Level 20 Player*

"Wink Girl?" I call out.

"Hey Cami!" She sheaths her swords and walks over to me, smiling.

"You look different."

She laughs. "Yeah, I changed my hair. I went with blonde before because that's what Kickerz liked. This is my natural color."

Her new raven-colored locks are beautiful and I tell her so. "I like the way that you've tied your hair back with that pearl-studded headband."

She smiles. "Keeps the hair out of my face while I'm fighting. I decided to specialize after talking to my new trainer. I'm a Blade Dancer."

"That fighting style looks impressive. All whirling blades and leaping about between targets."

"I'm working out my anger."

"Yeah?"

"Sometimes words are simply not enough to express how I'm feeling, which is why I am beating up on training dummies."

"More problems with Kickerz?"

"Is 'ugh' an emotion? Because I feel it all of the time when I think about him." She sighs. "We are officially over."

"I'm sorry."

"It happens."

"Some people leave. That's not the end of your story. That's the end of their part in your story."

She purses her lips together in a weird smile.

"What?"

"A small part." She giggles.

"I'm missing something here, aren't I?"

"Yep. I think so."

I shake my head. "Well, so long as you're happy."

"I'm happy that I won't be seeing him again. Not for a long time."

"You chose the opposite faction, didn't you? To stay away from him for the next 20 levels?"

"All TOP MEN make their members choose Jenan. Made it easy to ally myself with Reme."

"You're looking for some PVP revenge?"

"No. Not at all. Revenge is beneath me." She pulls a sword out of its sheath and brandishes it. "Although accidents happen."

I grin. "Poor Kickerz. He won't know what hit him."

"Did I ever tell you how Kickerz and I met?"

"No."

"It's kinda mixed into my inscription story. Want to go grab a snack? I'll tell you about it."

"Um, sure," I say. "Food sounds good."

She giggles again. "It's funny you should say that. Guess the name of the cafe I found."

"It's Food, isn't it?"

"Yep. The owners are players. And very straightforward. I had breakfast there this morning. A Dried Cherry Salad with Sugared Walnuts. So good."

We walk a few blocks and take a seat at one of the round, marble-topped outdoor tables. There are a few other people sitting in the area. All NPCs. A waitress comes to take our order. We get the special of the day, Fried Cakes with Sweet Cream and Strawberries. Wink Girl orders a double ristretto venti organic triple chocolate brownie iced vanilla double-shot caramel cappuccino, extra hot with foam whipped cream, upside-down blended. I order tea.

In a matter of moments our meal appears on the table. The waitress smiles at us without warmth as she asks if we would like anything else. It's the smile of someone who knows it's her job to smile at customers. Not insincere, but not friendly either. Professional. That's the word. It's a professional smile.

"When I was fifteen years old I was in a bad car accident," Wink Girl begins. "My friend's mother was behind the wheel. Becky, my friend, and her little sister were in the back seat. I had called 'shotgun' because I wanted to work the radio and was in the passenger side front seat. The car got t-boned just behind the front axel. Right at my door.

"My injuries were severe. I was knocked out. I wasn't breathing. I don't remember it, but my mom told me they cut me out of the wreck with the jaws of life. Rushed me to the ER." She takes a bite of a strawberry.

"I had persistent tachycardia, which is a fancy term for an abnormal heart rate. My heart rate was all over the place. I remember when I woke up in the hospital one of the first times I joked with my mom that that heart-rate machine they keep by the bed had a readout that looked like a lie detector test. She didn't really like that joke. Not sure why. I thought it was hilarious. Of course, it might have been whatever drugs they were pumping into my body at the time made a lot of things funny.

The crash broke my hip and bruised my heart. Or did I have bruises on my heart? In my heart? I can't remember. I had a severe concussion and double vision for a while. But the worst injury happened to my spine. Injuries from the crash severed my first and second vertebrae, which meant that my skull and spine were not connected. I was paralyzed from the neck down." She uses the fork to spread the cream over more of her fried cake.

"It was a very dramatic thing to wake up to. I tried to put a good face on for my parents. I didn't want them to be any more stressed than they already were, but it was difficult to deal with. It's scary to be in that situation.

"Along with the internal injuries, I had some external as well. My hip bone … I'm not sure what that's called. Technically or medically I mean. I just call it a hip bone. Anyway, the broken bone tore through the surface of my skin. The right side of my face was cut up from the glass shattering during the accident. On the plus side, I couldn't feel any pain, except for the cuts on my face.

"And in my mouth. My mouth was always dry for some reason. So dry it hurt."

I take a sip of tea, grateful that I can drink whenever I want in the Realms. Wink Girl's comments remind me of all the times back in the real world that Alby and I went thirsty because we were afraid of drinking inscribed water. That's the irony of the situation. The Hydrologists have created such wonderful things in the Realms. Fantastic marvels that surpass any other human invention. But if they hadn't started meddling with the water in the first place, if they hadn't started inscribing people, if they hadn't created the Aquariums with their fatal flaws, the world I grew up in wouldn't have been destroyed.

"The doctors wanted my parent's permission to try and reattach my skull to my spine so it wouldn't do further damage. There was only a fifty-fifty chance of surviving the surgery. And even if it worked, I would never walk again, never move any body part again.

"That was a bleak moment. And that was when the hydrologists from A Single Drop approached my parents. Convinced them that I could live a full, happy life with inscription.

"My parents couldn't afford life in an Aquarium, but the hydrologist sold them on the Realms. It was a brand-new idea, he said, and a lot cheaper. But even so, they could only get me an entry level package. No Homestead or other perks.

"They sold everything to get the money, including our house. It sold fast because it was in a gated community. Everyone wants a safe place to live."

"The riots hadn't started where you lived?"

"There were a few on the news, I guess. But not where we lived in California. Not like what was happening in the other countries. Anyway, I didn't want to be inscribed without them, but they just couldn't afford three entries. They're going to join me once they earn enough money to be inscribed.

"You're lucky you didn't go into the Aquariums," I said. "Most of them broke during the riots."

"They broke?"

"You didn't know?"

"No. We don't get news about the outside world in here."

"Yeah. I've noticed that. I kinda miss TV, even the news. We would watch the national news after dinner." How much should I tell her? How much will she believe? If I did the math right, which is always a bit iffy given my grasp of the subject, she would have entered the Realms about a year before the final collapse of the U.S. Would anyone who didn't live through it believe the horrific state of the real world?

"Yuck. I like reality shows better. It would be fun to watch something like that in the Realms."

"Or movies."

"Romantic comedies."

"No. SciFi epics. Other worlds. Time Travel. Or superhero movies."

"Superhero movies are the bomb!" We grin at each other.

"The villains always get the best lines in those movies."

"Yeah, that should change. Equal rights for heroes."

"Absolutely." I take a sip of tea. "Do you talk to your parents? You know, through the in-game email?"

"A bit. That was a sticky point for my parents. There's very little communication between the world outside of the Realms and players because it's so expensive. But my parents realized that I would be better off in here. And they will be able to join me later."

"So you haven't talked with them in a few years? You just send emails?"

"Yeah. Every three months I would go to MidWorld and talk to them. The hydrologists have a way to communicate with the real world via some sort of phone system. I think. I don't understand the technology. That's uber expensive, though. I don't want them wasting their money. I want them to be able to purchase their way into the Realms as soon as possible. So we stopped talking by phone. Except for once a year. But it's not ..." she hesitates. "It's not forever. Right? I'll see them again."

I take another sip of tea, trying to buy some time.

"What aren't you telling me?" Wink Girl narrows her eyes.

"I don't want to worry you."

She leans forward, grabbing my hand. "I respect people who tell me the truth. No matter how bad it is."

# Chapter Twenty

I take a deep breath and go for it. "I entered the Realms about six months ago. At that time, most of the Aquariums had broken. The inscribed water had reentered the water table. The inscribed human minds basically poison the water in the real world. If you drink it, your mind might be taken over by the inscribed one. Most …" I swallow hard. "Most people die after that unless they can flush the inscribed minds out of their systems."

Wink Girl recoils a little, eyes widening as if she has been slapped. "Why didn't the government …"

"Most of the governments fell right away. Rioting and terrorism. But the U.S. was one of the last countries to fall. Maybe your parents are okay."

Her lips thinned to a white line, her skin as pale as milk. "No wonder they don't tell us anything. They don't want us to know anything is wrong."

"The Hydrologists?"

"Yeah. Six months ago I stopped getting email messages. I made myself wait for a month. Then I went to MidWorld and asked. And they lied to me. And kept lying to me. Those m************ lied to me!" She thumps the table with her fist.

I grab the floral arrangement before it can topple to the ground.

She struggles to compose herself. The rims of her eyes are red. "I'm not going to cry."

"Okay. That's good. But there's nothing wrong with crying—"

"Don't be nice to me," she interrupts. "Or I'll lose it."

"Okay."

We sit quietly for a few moments. Then she yells "f***" at the top of her lungs. The other guests look in our direction, frowning and shaking their heads.

"Wait, what?" Wink Girl tips her head. "That sounded weird. You still have your curse blocker on?"

"Yeah."

"Oh come on, Cami." Her voice breaks and she clears her throat. "How am I supposed to express outrage if I can't swear?"

"Don't blame me. This is an area that young players can visit. So the curse blocker is automatically on. Still I think that people in the next town know you're ticked off."

A strained smile forces past her lips. "Don't try to make me laugh either."

"Okay." My voice is quiet. "My new trainer substitutes regular words that just sound naughty. It might work for you too."

"You mean like 'carp' instead of '****'?" Her smile becomes less strained. More natural. "It's something, I suppose."

"My dad used to say 'drunken fool' or 'feathers' when he was mad at something. Not really mad, you know. Just ticked off." I hadn't thought about this for a while. He never cursed. Not in front of us. Do some parents in the real world have voluntary curse blockers? I'll have to tell Alby about that idea. It will make her giggle.

She stands up. "I need to go beat up on a few targeting dummies again. I'll have to finish my story later. About meeting Kickerz." She clears her throat. "And you can tell me more about what happened in the world after I left." She takes out a handful of coins.

"I got the meal today." I say. "No worries."

"Thanks." Her lip quivers and her voice rises in pitch. I can tell she's trying not to cry. "Stay and finish. The food is good."

"Yeah, thanks for showing me this place."

"Don't mention it." She walks back in the direction of the thieves' training area.

After Wink Girl leaves, I pick at my food for a while. I don't feel hungry, although it's delicious. I keep thinking about her parents, about my dad. It makes me sick to think about what is happening in the world, way down in the pit of my stomach, but I think about it anyway. How many people have died because of what the Hydrologists created? How many could be saved by coming here, not as NPC slaves, but as Players? The Hydrologists have plans to open new realms, to encircle the entire globe. Why can't everyone be welcomed in to this new world?

Life in the Realms is so much fun, so fascinating, that I go along from day to day without thinking too much, simply driven by the adventure. Then something like my conversation with Wink Girl happens and it makes me wonder about the bigger picture. I need to learn more about the Hydrologists and their plans. That knowledge may be essential for the survival of my little family.

But I also need to focus on the game. On the quests. Gaining experience. Earning money and getting supplies. That's essential too.

"You eat like a man deprived of food for a lunar cycle."

I look up and see two level 100 NPCs dressed in the local style military uniform at a nearby table. Both have the type of glimmer surrounding them that is associated with a quest objective. Sort of a light silver sparkle. Once I notice them the sparkle disappears.

Plates of food cover the table where the male NPC sits. The female stands next to him. She seems somewhat amused. The AI identifies them as First Officer Sertaiven Gesahe and Lieutenant Jei Shum of the Neutram City Guard. Alignment neutral.

"Seeing death has a way of doing that to me. There were twenty bodies on that Woedboran airship we found. I mean, what's going on around here? We got almost continuous skirmishes breaking out with Jenan and Reme on one side, pirates at work on the other. You ask me, the world is going to heck-in-a-hand-basket."

"You fill in the Commander yet?" She frowns.

"Handed him the report myself. That makes the third time in a month raiders have hit an airship in this sector. They're getting bolder."

"And a lot more powerful. Their new weapons are doing more damage than anything they have used before. I wish we knew what type of weapons they have."

"Any idea where they might hit next? Any patterns?" Sertaiven picks up a pastry and takes a large bite.

"None that I can discern. The thing is, flight plan records are kept secret so the airships can avoid being attacked like this."

"It sounds as if there is a leak."

"I'm checking into it now."

"Good. Keep me informed." He gestures to the table. "Help yourself before you go. It's all terrific."

Jei snags a pastry. "Thanks."

"Don't mention it." He attacks the food with gusto as she walks away.

Time to make a choice. Should I follow her and try to learn more through observation? Should I sit and watch him eat, hoping for another person to wander over and provide more information. Or should I take the direct approach?

Yeah, right. If there was ever any choice.

I leave a few coins on the table to pay the bill and walk over to his table. "Hi."

"Hello." A guarded change comes over his feature when he notices my approach. Unless you were studying him closely, though, you wouldn't notice the shift. "Can I help you, citizen?"

"I think I may be able to help you. May I join you for a moment?"

He waves at the empty chair at his table. "Take a seat."

"I overheard your conversation with the other officer ..." I begin.

"Eavesdropping eh?" Something full of mischief flicks far back in his eyes and his face stretches into a wide smile. "Enamored of my looks? Or my sparkling personality? At least you admit it."

"It's not eavesdropping if you have the conversation outside in a public area," I argue.

"True. And quite frankly it's a strange expression, no? There isn't an eve in sight. Why would that be the first question that comes to my mind?"

I'm not sure how to respond and I'm starting to wonder if I made the right choice when I approached him. "I don't know."

He smiles then, and a bit of kindness creeps into his voice. "Don't worry about my nonsense. State your business."

"Cami."

"I'm sorry?"

"My name is Cami."

"Oh, I thought you were trying to sell me underwear."

"What?" Oh. Cami. Camisole. Yeah, not funny. "It's short for Camille."

He inclines his head. "You're not used to this, are you?"

"What's that?"

"Flirting?"

"Is that what we're doing?"

He chuckles. "I flirt with most adult females. Don't take it personally."

This is the strangest conversation I've been a part of recently. And honestly that's saying something.

"What's your name?" I ask even though the AI supplied it. I figure it will be less awkward if he tells me.

"First Officer Sertaiven Gesahe. At your service." He lingers on the last few words suggestively.

"Chargie, weh yuh deh pon?" A man walking up the street waves and grins at us. The language is strange, but somehow the meaning comes through as a suggestive "hey there, how're you doing?" One of the benefits of eating in an outdoor cafe is being part of the scenery. Being part of the spectacle of life. Random passersby will talk about you, or to you.

"You're very popular." I raise an eyebrow.

"That's meant for you."

"Luk gud." The passerby, a level 25 player named Gyalis from the guild Old Timers, tips me a wink and continues on his way.

"See?"

"I don't recognize the language," I admit, "although I understand what he meant."

"We get all sorts here. I met him last week. He says he's from somewhere called Jamaica, although I've never seen that on any map."

"Me either." I'm sure I must have studied that when I was in school in the real world, but I can't remember too much about geography. Was it a tropical island? Or rather, is it? I have to remember that those places from the real world still exist. At least until the Hydrologists finalize their plans.

"Of course we don't get many of your type in the city."

"Fae?" I ask.

"Stunningly beautiful women."

Oh right. Apparently, we're still flirting. I hate the fact that a blush has crept up my neck and over my face. He's handsome enough in his uniform, I guess, with rather strong features and close-cropped hair, but I am certainly not looking for romance.

"Do you ever think about anything except flirting?"

"Sometimes." He tips his head. "But I don't like to think about that when I'm eating."

Okay then. "When you are finished with your meal, I have some information you might find helpful."

"And what will it cost me?"

"Cost?" I frown.

"You're not selling information?"

Am I supposed to charge him? Is that how players earn money in the Traveler's Zone? It didn't work that way in the Starter Zone, where the money was paid out as a quest reward.

Since I don't know for certain, I decide to follow the familiar game pattern for now. "No. I'm not selling anything."

*Congratulations! Amity with Neutram City Guard increased by 100. Alignment: Neutral.*

"Okay. Unusual. But okay." He nods. "Go ahead."

"When you and the other officer were talking, you said you wanted to know about how the pirates brought down the Woedboran airship. I witnessed the battle."

# Chapter Twenty-One

"You witnessed the battle?" In an instant Sertaiven transforms. His previously friendly, flirtatious voice goes low and steady. Something shifts in his spine and shoulders, conveying a sense of steel and strength. And his eyes change. The mischievous sparkle transforms into a freezing cold beam. "From where?"

"I was in the forest."

"Really? Doing what?"

"Picking flowers."

"Flowers?"

"Two of my family members are attending the Professionum Scholae. They are studying to be alchemists, but they are too young to go out and gather materials. So I'm doing it for them."

"I've heard of the school," he says, a bit of the intensity leaving his gaze. "Good place to study?"

"The best in the world." Actually, it's the only school for young players, so technically it's the top.

He nods, the frown line between his eyes deepening a bit. "Go on."

"The people who attacked the ship were fire mages. They flew on some type of gliders. Strange ones with flapping wings."

"How many?"

"Five, I think. That's what I saw."

"What were the mages wearing?"

"They had robes. Sort of dark grey colored. Underneath they had tunic full of knotted tassels and colorful, geometric patches. The men wore black trousers and the woman a black skirt."

"You could see all of that from the ground?"

"Yes. And after they landed."

He places his hands on the table and leans toward me. "After?"

I'm a bit surprised at the force he puts into that question. "After the ship exploded and crashed, I went to see if there were any survivors."

"Must have been a lot of smoke and flame."

"There was. But I'm fae. We can heal people."

"Magic?"

"Yes."

He leans back, still holding my eyes with his steady gaze. "Good to know. So were there?"

"What?"

"Any survivors?"

"Yes. One. The Ambassador." I didn't hesitate. I had decided before I came to the table to tell this man the truth. Is this a mistake? I don't know, but I have to trust the quest path to steer me in the right direction.

"So Finn survived. I'm glad to hear it." A bit of the tension leaves his face.

"I hope so. I healed him to the best of my ability. He said he would go to the GreenWood for further help."

He nods. "And then?"

"Well, three of the pirates survived. A woman named Cheville and two men named Murry. They approached our position, so I circled around to lead them away from Finn."

"You circled ..." his voice fades and he clears his throat. "Go on."

"And I overheard them discussing Finn. They attacked the ship to kill him. They needed proof of death to get paid."

"You overheard all of this without getting caught? And you just brought it to me out of the kindness of your heart?"

"Yes, I—"

"You're one of the Travelers right? Here for just a bit. Make a big splash and then leave. Get your gold and whatever and you're gone. No ties. No loyalty."

"I don't know that term." But I realize that I do. When I first arrived in the Realms the Forrest Guardians greeted me with the expression "What ho, Traveler." And this is the Traveler's Zone, after all. Is that how the Hydrologists have described us to the NPCs that live here? That we're just traveling through? So they don't ask too many questions when we leave and the next round of players comes through.

And really, isn't that what we're doing? Coming in and doing the quests, earning our rewards, and then moving on once we level? Part of the world, but never really part of the community.

"I don't know how long I'm going to be here," I say. "No one knows how long they have anywhere in this world. But we do have control over what we do when we're here. That's really what it comes down to. And I choose to try and help."

*Quest Complete! It Only Seems Impossible Until It's Done.*

*Reward:* **Nightfall.** *Experience Gained.*

*Congratulations Player! You have reached Level 21.*

*You receive a 1% bonus to intellect, strength, spirit, and agility.*

*Congratulations player! You have learned the spell:* **Nightfall**

*Cast Time: 1 Second*

*Mana Cost: 20 Points*

*By channeling the power of the Dark Star, this spell causes an object to radiate darkness out to a 50 yard radius. Lasts for 10 minutes or until dispelled.* **Nightfall** *causes the illumination in the area to drop one level. Thus bright light becomes normal light; normal light becomes shade; shade becomes darkness. Non-magical items like lanterns do not brighten an area effected by* **Nightfall**. *This* *spell has no effect in an area that is already dark.*

The Dark Star? I mentally sigh. Another item to add to my list of random things I need to find out about eventually. 50 yards is huge. Half the size of a football field. I wonder if it's moveable? If I cast it on myself will it travel with me when I walk? What kind of advantage does this offer? I suppose it might help me sneak up on people. But wouldn't they notice when the light suddenly goes away?

I would notice. So would Alby and L.G. But I can think of quite a few people I've met who wouldn't even question if the sky went from day to night at high noon.

Sertaiven interrupts my thoughts by smiling. "Maybe you're okay. Maybe you can be of use."

*Congratulations! Amity with Neutram City Guard increased by 100. Alignment: Friendly.*

"How?"

He glances over at the other diners. Some of them have been watching our little drama curiously. He lowers his voice. "We do have some security issues here. I'm guessing you haven't been in town long. But your arrival might be … timely."

*Quest Offered: It Only Seems Impossible Until It's Done II*

*Difficulty May Vary.*

*Reward: Unknown. Yes/No?*

"Yes."

I'm not sure if Sertaiven is aware of the quest being offered or not. I find it interesting both ways. If he's aware, then the NPCs in the Traveler's Zone have more knowledge than they admit. If he doesn't know what's going on, then there is a whole level to the world that is beyond their knowledge.

He stands up and claps me on the shoulder. "Let's get going. Time to meet the Commander." He places a few coins on the table.

"Don't you want to take the rest of the food with you?" I ask.

"No way to carry it. And I don't want to wait for the waitress to bring a carrier."

I feel bad for interrupting his meal. There are a lot of pastries left. "I can carry it for you." I pat my **Bag of Infinite Holding**.

"That's one of those magic bags? Sure, if you have room." He stares as the food disappears from my hand. "Those are useful."

"Don't they sell bags in town? I'm sure I saw a shop."

He chortles. "For about half of my year's salary."

I never thought about what expenses the NPCs might have. Interesting. This reinforces my idea that most of them don't know about the quests. Otherwise they would have to carry money designated for the quest rewards. And items given as rewards. Where would they get the money? Would it just mysteriously appear in their bags and then disappear each time a player turns in a quest? What if they didn't have a bag?

Of course, some NPCs know. Tanyl, for instance. And Myke. But this isn't the time for musing. A tall, regal-looking human NPC, dressed in orate robes accented with an unseemly amount of gold braid and filigree, greets Sertaiven as we leave the restaurant. He has dark, glittering eyes and hair that is deep black. The AI identifies him as Caius Egnatius Quatruus, Ambassador to the Reme Empire.

"Mr. Gesahe. How wonderful to see you!"

"Ambassador." He tries to continue on his way, but the larger man steps in front of him.

"Aren't you going to introduce me to your charming companion?"

"No." Sertaiven says firmly.

Short and sweet. I like it.

"If she wants to introduce herself to you, she will."

I bite my lip to hide a smile.

"You know your problem, Mr. Gesahe? You're not a people person."

"Ambassador! Ambassador!"

Another NPC identified as Lars Ulpius Pantera, diplomatic attaché of Reme, runs down the street toward our group. His robes are precisely like the ones Caius wears, if not quite as gilded. His outfit also has a few loose threads and stains.

"Ah, have you met the newest member of my diplomatic staff? Just arrived from Reme."

"Ambassador!" The younger man's face gleams with sweat.

"Yes, Lars. What is it?"

"Our agricultural district? Imbinare? In the north?"

"Yes, I know where it is. What about it?"

"It's under attack. No provocation. No warning." He gasps for breath and continues.

"They are firing on anything that moves. Airships. All of our defenses are down."

"Who launched the attack?"

"I don't know. No one does."

# Chapter Twenty-Two

"You're going to need to speak to the Commander. And quickly." As the Ambassador and his attaché rush away Sertaiven starts walking in the opposite direction. "If there has been an incident, he will be occupied trying to broker a diplomatic solution between Reme and Jenan. He won't have time to deal with pirate attacks."

"I thought Lars said no one knows who attacked?"

"It has to be Jenan. No one else would have the firepower to overcome Reme's defenses. Even a small town like Imbinare is fortified beyond belief. It's one of the reasons that communities join the Empire. Their level of protection against raiders is second to none."

I follow him through the streets, which have emptied somewhat in the heat of the day. Occasionally he exchanges a greeting, but for the most part people move out of his way.

"This city is huge."

"This your first time here?"

"Yep."

"It can be a bit confusing until you get the lay of the land."

"Stop! Stop! Thief!"

Sertaiven swerves, crossing the road to intercept an elderly woman standing by a community well. She is yelling and pointing down an alley.

"Good morning, Mistress Lydia. Bit of trouble?"

"He took my bucket. Ripped it out of my hands." She's clutching her arm at the wrist. Blood stains the sleeve.

I cast **Slow Heal**. She blinks owlishly in my direction.

"Thank you, young lady."

"I see." Sertaiven takes out a note pad and pencil.

"What are you going to do about it, young man! I'm a tax payer. I have rights!"

"I shall be pursuing him momentarily. Can you provide a description?"

"One of those outsiders. A Traveler. Wearing a black jerkin."

"Ah." Sertaiven closes the note pad and places it back in his pocket. "I know exactly where to go. Excuse me, mistress."

"And me, a widow-woman. Shouldn't need to haul water. But I do. Else how do I get water? You tell me that!" She yells after us.

"Are you going to chase the thief?"

"No point. I know where he's going." He turns into an alley so narrow that it is barely visible. I squeeze in after him. It's full of the echoing sounds of our steps, our voices, our breathing. The light filters grudgingly from above, sneaking in between the two buildings in a thin, dazzling beam.

"Most people don't know about this short cut," Sertaiven says in a conversational tone. "They think that the only way to get from Main Street to Fellowship Row is to go down to the other end of Hillcrest Road around Welsh Park. But you can, because you're able to squeeze through these cement posts. And here we are in Fellowship Alley. Right between the two oldest Guild houses, TOP MEN and Waterford."

He stops at the end of the alley, staying in the shadows.

"What are we waiting for?"

"The right moment."

There is the sound of running feet. Sertaiven takes a quick step out, swinging a small baton into the chest of a player. He stops dead, falling, and starts twitching. The AI identifies him as Waifulover, a level 21 thief. The bucket of water drops and the liquid spreads over the cobbles. On the bottom, burned into the wood, is the phrase 'Property of M. Lydia."

"It's a **Zap Stick**. Very effective," Sertaiven says as he yanks Waifulover to his feet. He pulls out a whistle and blows it with three short bursts. "We'll soon sort this out."

A few black tunic wearing players come out of the TOP MEN guild hall.

"Hey. You aren't supposed to do that!" a level 30 player named Soggie Noodles protests. He moves towards Sertaiven, who points the **Zap Stick** in warning.

There are sounds of hurrying feet on the street. Several Neutram City Guards rush up behind us. They are also armed with **Zap Sticks**.

"She's with me," Sertaiven barks at the guards.

I'm grateful he identifies me. Some of them had been eying me, and they are also Level 100 NPCs.

Waifulover is still twitching and drooling a bit as Sertaiven hands him off to one of the others. "Cuff him so he can't work any of his tricks and take him to the Stockade. He's got a date before the Commander."

"You can't take him away!"

"Watch me."

"But you're a guard."

"I know that."

Soggie Noodles shakes his head. "Guild laws apply here. Not city laws."

"You see what this is?" Sertaiven points at the ground. "It's a city street. It doesn't belong to your guild."

"We'll see about that," Soggie Noodles sneers. He turns to his friends on the stairs. "Any of the admins about?"

"No, but the guild leader is here."

"Well get him! This is serious." He stares at Sertaiven. "He'll sort this out."

"Good. I'd like to see that."

It's a tense standoff. Yet the players don't leave the steps of their guild hall and the NPCs remain on the street. There must be a barrier. One I can't see because I'm not a member of their guild.

"Are the cuffs magic?" I ask to break the silence. They have a brilliant red glow, like the metal is heated from within. I haven't seen anything like them in the game before.

Seraiven nods. "They block any type of magic or other nonsense a suspect might use to try and escape."

My appreciation for the Hydrologists who designed this system increases. They have thought this through. "Seems like a sensible precaution."

The other player returns, panting a bit from running.

"Well?" Soggie Noodles says impatiently.

"He says to deal with it or he'll boot us from the guild."

"Right." Soggie Noodles sighs and points to Waifulover, whose eyes have started to focus again. "Dude, you failed the entry challenge. Guild rights and status revoked. Deal with the city law on your own."

The TOP MEN designation disappears from over Waifulover's head. That sobers him up in a hurry. "What the …? Come on dude! That challenge is messed up and you know it. If you let me put the bucket in my bag—"

"It wouldn't be a challenge if you magic away the evidence." Soggie Noodles sighs. "Don't you get it?"

"No." Waifulover frowns sullenly.

"You can re-apply again in six months. Until then, you're on your own."

"Get him out of here." Sertaiven orders the other guards. "Look sharp. And read him his rights. I want this legal."

One of the guards moves to pick up the bucket. Soggie Noodles makes a quick motion with his hands. A lance of ice shoots out, freezing the bucket to the ground. All of the TOP MEN gathered on the stairs laugh.

"Oops," Soggie Noodles says with exaggeration. "Sorry. Accidents happen."

"Take a few steps forward and try that."

Soggie Noodles just grins and holds up his hands. "Why would I want to do that, Mr. Guard? I'm safe here."

"For now."

Soggie Noodles turns his attention to me as the guards disperse. "What you looking at, scrub?"

"I thought all TOP MEN were thieves."

"We take all sorts. But not 'gurls.'" He smirks in my direction. "Females need to learn their place."

I can't believe I'm hearing such antiquated garbage. "There's no difference between men and women in the realms in terms of gear or stats. It's a totally equal playing field."

"Whatever." Soggie Noodles brushes me off with a flip of his hand. "No matter what you think, at the top of the chain it's a man's game."

I open my mouth to respond, and then stop. Why do I want to argue with an idiot? "Well, good luck with that."

My comment startles him. I think he wanted me to make an angry retort so he could play off of it. No, not just 'wanted' but needed to make me argue with him so he could feel superior. So he could get some of his pride back after losing face with the guards.

Yeah, good luck with that.

Sertaiven frowns with impatience and I turn to follow him. "We have to hurry to catch the Commander before he's called away to deal with the crisis."

Ducking down alleys and leaping over short walls, it is only a few minutes until we reach the center of the city. The streets are more crowded. We weave around merchants in brown and red tunics, humbler folk in homespun clothing, and a group of black-robed monks walking in procession to a nearby cathedral.

All this is new. All interesting. I'd love to stay and have a look. To explore the buildings. To find out about the people and places. But there's no time to pause. Even though I have a longer stride due to my fae height advantage, I'm finding it difficult to keep up with Sertaiven and break into a jog every few minutes. Soldiers and guards must have special training with walking at a fast pace without getting winded. Or they train. A lot.

"What's going to happen to him?" I ask when we reach the steps of a large building. It's impressive. Limestone, terra cotta, fieldstone, white brick, and sandstone mix to make a building that is part Victorian, part Gothic, and part Moorish.

"He'll be fined."

"What if he can't pay the fine?"

"He'll spend some time in the Stockade."

"How do you keep people in there? Locked-up?"

He pauses at the top of the steps, looking back at me curiously. "What do you mean?"

"Most people have **Residence Stones**."

"Ah. Those magic transport stones Traveler's all carry? Yeah, those don't work in the Stockades."

Right. I remember what the AI said about that earlier. "They only work in certain areas of the city?"

"Part of the city charter. Helps us uphold law and order."

Sertaiven holds the door for me. I don't think anyone has done that since my dad. A pang of melancholy strikes, short and sweet, and I take a moment to compose my emotions.

Of course I can open the door myself. That's not the point. It's the little gesture, little courtesy, that means so much. It's why I hold doors for Alby and L.G. Putting someone else's needs, someone else's comfort, in front of your own. It's instinctive, or at least it should be.

So many Players have the "me first" vision of life. But an equal number of NPCs have the opposite view. Did someone create them to be that way? One of the Hydrologists? Or is that something that happened naturally in the course of the game? I add this thought to my ever-growing list of things to learn about in the future.

Sertaiven walks up to a woman seated behind a desk and begins speaking to her in low, earnest tones. I get my opportunity to look around as they debate. Stained glass windows, propped open to allow a cross breeze, a tin roof, and hand-drawn stencil ornamentations catch my attention. The furniture looks like it has existed for generations, all leather and varnished, hand-carved wood.

Sertaiven seems to have won his argument. "Wait here." He motions to one of the leather couches. "I'll be back in a few moments."

I sit next to two level 22 dwarf players identified as Sky Strike and Thunderfury who are having an animated discussion.

"Well, isn't this just perfect. Called before the Commander!"

"How was I supposed to know it's illegal?"

"Just shut up and help me think." Sky Strike holds up a hand. "On second thought, just shut up. It's your thinking that got us into this mess in the first place."

"But it's a quest for Reme," Thunderfury argues, a bit of whine creeping into his tone. "They have to respect the quest!"

"You think they care? It's a different city. Different rules." Sky Strike rubs his hand through a beard that would do any two dwarves proud. "OK, this is pointless. We need to come up with some kind of lie they will believe."

Several NPCs scurry about. A young man hurries past holding a sheaf of papers, looking as if he is haunted by the documents he carries.

Sertaiven returns. "Come on. Commander Platt is waiting."

The Commander is dressed in a similar uniform to Sertaiven. Older, but not far past his prime. His short hair is speckled with grey. He beckons me forward. The hand that takes my own is the hand of a worker, not soft but strong.

The office is a pleasant place. It is paved with terra cotta tiles and has plastered walls painted with murals depicting bird's eye views of the city. Unlike the reception area, the windows in this room are closed. No eavesdropping possible.

"It's an honor to meet you. Camille, isn't it?" He waves at the chair in front of his desk. "Please, have a seat. Can I get you anything to eat or drink?"

"No. Thank you, sir."

"Call me Marcus." He takes his own seat and folds his hands on the desk. "First Officer Gesahe has informed me of your adventures today."

"I'd like to help, but I'm not sure what else I have to offer."

# Chapter Twenty-Three

"Have you encountered the race known as Polyperibitians?"

I shake my head. "I don't think so. I haven't been in this area for long. This is the first city I've visited."

"You won't see many of them in the city."

"You'd know if you did." Sertaiven leans casually against the wall opposite the Commander's desk. "They're tall. Taller even than you. And they're vicious fighters. Three arms. Pure muscle. Usually armed to the teeth."

A glimmer starts to form in the back of my mind. That last battle in Tanyl's Training Room with the unknown constructs— But my train of thought is interrupted as the Commander continues.

"The Polyperibitians are a race renowned for fighting, as Sertaiven notes, and are justifiably proud of their prowess in battle. They hail from Vastnen, a distant land destroyed ages ago in a catastrophe that, from all accounts, ripped their land asunder and sank it beneath a mountain of flame and ash."

Game lore. Even though the narrative is created by the Hydrologists, it's real to these people. I won't be as quick to dismiss it this time. I nod and wait for him to continue.

"After they lost their homeland, they wandered for a while and encountered many different civilizations. This didn't improve their general disposition."

"They grew more fierce and hostile than ever," Sertaiven adds.

"They have resettled in the Wild Lands, in a northern valley and, according to our scouts, have carved out a fairly comfortable existence. And some of the Polyperibitians have branched out. Offered their services to other races—"

"Mercenaries for hire."

Commander Platt briefly glances at his First Officer, then continues. "They're even open to trade negotiations. Mostly due to the influence of their leader's eldest son, Shaer Prein. He's a bit more progressive than his father and sees the value in establishing diplomatic channels."

"Trade or diplomacy?" I ask.

"In this case they are the same."

"I see, I think."

He leans forward, steepling his hands reflectively. "We're sending an airship tomorrow to the Polyperibitians's main village. An offering of goods from Neutram. And a member of the diplomatic core will accompany the shipment to smooth things over. Perhaps sign a treaty or two."

"If they're allied with Neutram, they won't be as quick to take sides with either Reme or Jenan."

This earns Sertaiven a direct stare from Commander Platt. "Yes, exactly."

I look back and forth between them. "What does this have to do with me?"

"I'd like you to go along tomorrow as a formal Advisor to the Neutram Ambassador. It won't take long, and you might even find it enjoyable."

"Explore strange places. Meet new people." Sertaiven grins.

"New people armed to the teeth," I say. "You're expecting an attack, and want to know if it's the same people who attacked the Woedboran airship."

"You'll be safe," Sertaiven adds quickly. "Since we're expecting trouble, we've taken precautions."

No matter how cautious they are, the people on that ship can still die. But they might have a better chance of survival if I go. And I might find out more information about the pirates and why they have mage abilities that should be limited only to players. Who could change that about the NPCs and why would they want to?

Once again I feel, not a thrill, that's not the right word, but a sense of anticipation. As if the answer is right there waiting for me to figure it out. As long as no one else has to die.

Myke is right. The choices are less clear the further I progress into the game. If I didn't go and none of them came back, it would eat at me forever. I would not be able to live with myself, wondering if I could have made a difference.

"Will you accept?"

*Quest Offered: Fair Winds, Fair Trade*
*Difficulty May Vary.*
*Reward: Unknown. Yes/No?*

"Yes," I respond, both to the Commander and to the AI.

"Splendid!

"Just to be clear, I'm not in charge of anything. I'm going as an observer. I'm happy to join in the fighting to save the ship from the pirates, if it comes to that, but no one will live or die on my command." Even as I say it, my discomfort grows. Is the game setting me up to face a situation that I want to avoid? And if I need to defend the airship, it might mean killing pirate NPCs.

Commander Platt arches an eyebrow. "We generally don't trust strangers with command."

"We save that for the second date." Sertaiven tips me a wink.

"I see."

"Thank you, Camille. I will make certain the Captain and the Ambassador will know of your appointment. Be at the main city dock tomorrow at dawn."

I can use the quest line to find it, so I'm not worried about the location, but I'm curious. "What's the name of the ship?"

"The Stormherald. Captained by Nyrie Balere. One of the most seasoned officers in our fleet."

"I look forward to meeting her." I stand and shake hands with the Commander.

Sertaiven steps quickly to the door and holds it open. "Please wait outside for a moment. I need to have a quick word with my boss."

I nod and walk back, taking a seat on the leather couch opposite the two dwarf players. Sky Strike and Thunderfury are still arguing.

"I'm not going to follow your lead. Every time you come up with something, you end up making things worse."

"Oh please. When have I ever steered you wrong?" Thunderfury's voice goes up a notch.

"Um, the last dungeon run we went on ring a bell? The one with the guy pretending he was a moose?"

"How do you know he wasn't?"

"How do I know he wasn't a moose? Is that what you're asking? Um, maybe the fact that he was wearing a moose costume!"

"Ah, but how do you know he wasn't a moose wearing a fake moose costume to throw us off the fact that he was a moose underneath? Huh? Riddle me that, Riddler!"

I can't take it anymore. "Excuse me."

Their attention snaps in my direction. "Well, hello, pretty lady."

"So nice to meet a fellow player here."

Their voices ooze fake charm. I try not to shudder visibly. "I couldn't help overhearing you before. When you were wondering what to tell the Commander."

"Yes?"

"What about the truth? He probably knows it anyway."

"But that's ..." Sky Strike's voice trails off.

"You think he does?" Thunderfury's face is a mask of concern.

I shrug. "You've been sitting here talking about what lie you can tell to smooth it over. Make it okay." I wave my hand. "In this public place. With all of the Commander's people wandering about. With his receptionist sitting a few feet away. I could be wrong, but I bet he has a clue."

They stare at me blankly for a moment. Then Sky Strike slaps the back of his hand against Thunderfury's arm.

"Ow!"

"This is all your fault."

"How is this ALL my fault?"

"Dude ..."

As soon as the door to the Commander's office opens, I'm on my feet. I don't want to hear round three.

"That anxious to see me?" Sertaiven smiles.

"Can we go someplace quieter?"

"Of course." He leads me to a room farther down the hall. "My office is your office."

The room is a smaller version of Commander Platt's office, with a lot more paper stacked in piles on the desk and side tables.

The amount of clutter impresses me. "How do you find anything?"

"I know exactly where everything is." He taps his finger against his temple. "Mind like a steel trap."

I smile. "Do you remember why you asked me to wait here?"

"A couple of things. First, to make sure that you actually want to go on this adventure. You seemed a bit hesitant back there. If you're afraid of combat—"

"No. I'm not. In fact I have trained so much in the last year I'm looking forward to putting those skills to the test. And I want to be helpful. To be useful. But I don't want other people to die because of something I did."

"Sounds a bit like survivor's guilt."

"I don't know what that is."

"You know. You live when someone else dies. You feel guilty about it, although it really isn't your fault. Soldiers face this more often than I care to think about …" His voice fades away. "Hey, are you okay? You've gone awfully pale."

Images rush over me. Our kitchen in the real world. The Hydrologist in my father's body. The ravages of dehydration. The gun in my hand. The blood splattering over the wall, over the refrigerator, obscuring the pictures Alby had made with the colored sand.

I can't think about this. I won't. Focus on anything else. On Alby. On L.G. On our new house and the garden we are planning. On absolutely anything else.

"I'm fine. Just a little tired." It isn't much of a lie. I could use a good nap since I haven't been sleeping much. "But I'll be ready for tomorrow. Ready to help bring justice for the Woedborans and hopefully set up trade between Neutram and the Polyperibitians."

"Lofty goals."

"Absolutely." I manage to smile. "So what's the second thing?"

"Hmm?" He's still studying my face, a little frown of worry creasing his forehead right between his eyes.

"You said there were a couple of things ..." I let my voice trail off.

"Ah yes, I'd like my lunch, please, if it survived the trip in your magic bag."

I pull out the plate of pastries. "Where should I set them?"

"Oh, anywhere." He waves at the piles of papers. "Quite frankly, it doesn't matter. I never read those things anyway."

# Chapter Twenty-Four

After leaving Sertaiven's office, I head into the city to explore. Alby and L.G. will also enjoy looking around someplace new, but they're still in school for a few more hours. Until I can meet up with them, I'm on my own. I figure I can take a quick look around, maybe do a few simple quests, and then go outside the city to look for herbs and flowers for my two favorite alchemists.

This time I stroll the streets rather than dashing through the alleys. The buildings are impressive, mostly made of stone or brick. They are bigger than the homes in Old Town, a little grander in design, but still have a lived-in feeling. I spot a broken tile here, some chipped masonry there, and a few wilted flowers in window-boxes.

The market square had traditional stores as well as NPC merchants displaying their wares in stalls open to the street. They call out to catch the attention of every passerby, adding to the background noise of braying pack animals, children shrieking in play, and wandering minstrels.

"Elixirs and potions! The strongest of the strong!"

"The finest in mystic herbs and spices. Buy one get one at half  price!"

"Jewels here. The finest in jewels imported from far-off dwarf mines in the Wild Lands. Augment your gear with rare and unusual buffs!"

"Transmutes here! Get your transmutes here!"

So loud. I have to force myself not to cover my ears as I weave through the crowds. Everybody is very busy buying and selling. I'll have to remember to avoid this area in the future. My sister and L.G. will hate the noise as well.

There are street signs and markers, which help me to navigate. I see "Fellowship Row" and head in that direction, curious about the guild houses. I only caught a quick glimpse when Sertaiven arrested Waifulover. Most of my attention had been on the other players, and the guards, watching for that movement, that increase in tension, that would bring about violence.

I've never wanted to join a guild. I have enough trouble of my own navigating this world. I don't want the drama that other players bring. But I admit to being curious about how the other half lives. Why are they all so anxious to belong?

The houses are large but are not particularly impressive. They are made of the same materials as the other buildings. I wonder what makes them special? Why does the city law stop at the edges of their property?

The wooden bucket still lies on the cobbles in front of the TOP MEN. The ice has melted and it has an unusual glow. I walk over and pick it up by the handle.

*Quest Offered: A Drop in the Bucket.*

*Instructions: Return the item to its rightful owner.*

*Difficulty: Easy.*

*Reward: 1 Gold Piece. Yes/No?*

"Yes."

Thankfully this seems to be a quick quest. Something like the "rescue the kitty in the tree" type quests I did in the Starter Zone. I focus on the quest name and follow the GPS line through the streets. The path leads me past the well and I pause for a moment to fill the bucket with cold, clean water. It's a little harder to carry, but I feel sorry for Mistress Lydia. No one should ever have to go without clean water.

I arrive at a two-story weathered brick building. A wooden sign hung over the open door reads "Come Back Inn." A gust of breeze makes the sign swing gently on its wrought-iron support.

I have to duck under the low door frame. It isn't made for someone as tall as a fae. Fortunately, the ceilings are high enough that I don't smack my head.

The place has a pleasant musty smell, lacquered wide-plank wood floors, braided rag rugs, well-worn furniture, and paintings of various people and places. It's illuminated by lily sconce gaslights. My nose also catches the strong reek of fuel. At the back of this room sits an old-fashioned hotel desk with a call bell on it.

I ring the bell. Mistress Lydia enters from a back room. She stands with the desk between us.

"Can I help you, miss?"

"I brought back your bucket. I found it in the street." I decide not to go through the whole story with her. It would take too much time.

"Set it on the desk please."

*Quest Complete! A Drop in the Bucket.*

*Reward: 1 Gold Piece. Experience gained.*

*Congratulations! Amity with Mistress Lydia increased by 100. Alignment: Neutral.*

Mistress Lydia glances at the bucket and then spends more time looking me over. A long, frank, silent appraisal.

"You're the young lady who was with the guard. The one who healed me."

"Yes, my name is Cami." I stick out my hand and she shakes it.

A trickle of water leaks down the side of the bucket. Mistress Lydia catches a drop on her finger, staring at it as if fascinated. "You filled the bucket."

"Yes. I thought you would need the water. No one should ever go thirsty. I know what that's like. It's not fun."

*Congratulations! Thanks to your act of kindness, amity with Mistress Lydia increased by 500. Alignment: friendly. Each amity rank gained with NPCs provides rewards. New Ability: Converse freely.*

She stares at me with an expression I can't read. The silence stretches on for a few moments.

"Well, have a good day," I say, and turn toward the door.

"Young lady. Cami. Wait!" Mistress Lydia has come out from behind the desk. She grips my arm to stop me.

"Are you all right?" I ask.

"Yes. It's just … I want to warn you, but I don't know—" Her voice trails off and she releases her grip. "Maybe it's not necessary."

"Warn me about what?"

"I'm a widow. I have to earn a living. And running an inn isn't as profitable as it used to be because of those dang guilds. Nobody needs a room anymore. They just get rooms at the guild houses." She looks me in the eye, almost pleading. "I've got to earn a living."

"What are you talking about?"

"I'm not saying he made me do it, because he didn't. I took his coin, right enough. But now I see it weren't right." Her face changes, suddenly older and more tired. "Not by a long shot. He shouldn't be bothering a good girl like you."

There is something important here. Something I don't understand. I feel an almost adolescent fury of frustrated questions. "Please, Mistress Lydia. What are you saying?"

"That man. The guild leader of TOP MEN. He paid me money so that one of his recruits could steal my bucket. A test he says. A challenge."

"Okay. But what does this have to do with me?"

"He weren't testing the recruit. He were testing you, miss. He said he knows who you really are, but not what you're made of."

My hands start to tremble. "What do you mean?"

'He set it up, see, so that the recruit would steal my property when you walked by. He wants to see what you would do." She frowned. "I don't think he figured on the guard being with you."

A feeling of panic sweeps over me, but I work at keeping my expression calm. "Did he set up this return quest?"

"I don't know what you mean, miss."

Right. She probably doesn't know about the quests. Or she's a good actor. Or she's not allowed to acknowledge it. A limit put in by the Hydrologists. Does that make sense, or doesn't it? I take a deep breath to calm myself. I will have to consider this question carefully, and this isn't the time.

"Thank you, Mistress Lydia. I appreciate the warning." I turn to leave but stop at the door and look at her over my shoulder. "Just one more thing. Will you tell me the guild leader's name?"

"He said to call him Nemesis."

Of course. "Thank you. again."

I exit the inn, keeping my face a careful mask. I don't want to give anything away to my unknown observer. Nemesis, for heaven's sake. Other players and their goofy names. Only the hydrologists seem to take regular names like Brent, Darlene, and Susan. That might be some sort of a company rule so that a new player doesn't wake from inscription and have to interact with someone named Killer of Fluffy Things or Eorkkkkk.

So based on the name, my adversary is definitely a regular player, except ... I don't know if Nemesis is really his game name.

Only another player who has seen him could tell me that. NPCs just go with the name we tell them. They don't have access to the AI's additional information.

"A test," Mistress Lydia had said. And "he said he knows who you really are."

That phrase. I've read that phrase before. During my first few days in the realms, I received an anonymous threatening letter with the message "I know who you are. I know you're a fraud." The list of people who could have sent the letter to me is short: A Hydrologist or Michael, who gave me the password that let me enter into the Reams as a player rather than a slave.

Michael, who I recently saw in MidWorld crawling through the ventilation ducts. Who probably set off those explosions. Who seemed very interested in the tablet I accidentally stuck into my bag during the rush to escape MidWorld.

But if he is here, and set up as a player, why would he want to torment me? What would he have to gain?

And since I was inscribed before Michael, how could he be the guild master of TOP MEN? That guild was around the first day I started playing. Within hours of joining, Alby and I ran into that obnoxious player Farty McFart-pants who kept challenging me to a duel. He's a member of TOP MEN.

Michael couldn't be Nemesis. The timeline is wrong . . . unless he knows a way to enter and leave the game world at will.

When I was grabbed by the military and forced into the realms, the doctor who performed the procedure was trying to save the inscribed bodies from deteriorating into withered husks. He wanted to be able to perform re-inscriptions. To put inscribed minds back into human bodies rather than into the Aquariums or the Realms.

Is that possible? Could Michael be living in both the real and the virtual world? Spending time in the realms and then going back to his body? Where it's kept on some sort of life-support until he returns?

Too many questions! My brain is starting to hurt thinking about all the possibilities. And I don't have anyone to ask. Somehow I don't think this information is located in one of the in-game books.

So—options now. I could go to confront Nemesis at the guild house. But those areas have their own rules. Ones I don't know. They might have PVP set up as a standard option, like some of the battlegrounds. The players could be higher than me in level and gear score. And if I got into trouble, I couldn't just leave. The **Residence Stones** only work in the Portal Room, the inns, and the cathedral. I could be trapped in there with no way to escape.

Plus there's no guarantee he would see me. Why would he want to at this stage? It would ruin his game.

I exit the city and wander into the surrounding forest, taking deep breaths to try and calm my mind. I honestly want to charge right in to the TOP MEN guild house and force a reckoning with Nemesis, but that would be folly. I know this intellectually, but emotionally I'm off balance.

Be calm in every situation, my dad used to say. Train yourself. Excessive emotion in the face of danger accomplishes nothing.

Easier said than done.

So I concentrate on the here-and-now. What can I do that will be productive? That will help improve life for my family?

I haven't earned much money today, that's for sure. I should get busy and go herbing. That way I won't return empty-handed.

I shift to **Flightform** and take wing through the pine and spruce trees. In the shaded areas, moss carpets the trees, earth, stones, and fallen logs alike. Squirrels dart up the tall trees. I head for an area where bright sunshine filters through the evergreens and the trees have been cleared out.

Shifting back to my regular fae form, I emerge from the woods into a small field whose far end terminates in the granite grey rock of a mountain. In the grass I spot a tell-tale glimmer and find a plant with small, white flowers. I pick it immediately and receive new information from the AI.

*Congratulations! You have reached a new level of the Herbalism Skill. Current gathering level: Professional 1. Herbalism allows you to find and harvest herbs and plants scattered throughout the realm. It is a primary profession linked with the skills of alchemy and cooking, although herbs may be useful in other professions as well.*

*Upon reaching the Professional level, players have a 100% chance of gathering both flowers/plants and seeds.*

*Congratulations! Your knowledge is increasing. You have unlocked lore on Sweet Woodruff. Review: Yes/No?*

"Yes."

*Sweet Woodruff are classified as among the vast collection of flowers and herbs used for alchemy. Known for their strong medical properties, they are generally located in wooded areas and in lowlands. The flowers can be combined with other materials when using the alchemy skill. Alchemy will imbue the item with additional benefits. It can be used with success as a substitute for Mellow, Rue, and Knotgrass. No known use in cooking.*

*Warning: Large quantities of this plant can produce dizziness and symptoms of poisoning.*

Interesting. That's the second flower I've picked outside of the Starter Zone that mentions poisoning. Is this a pattern? How useful are poisons in the game? I will have to keep track and see.

I clear all of the flowers from this area. Thus far I have gathered an equal amount of flowers and seeds. At this rate I will be able to fill a large section of our planned garden. When the flowers and plants mature, Alby and L.G. will get a chance to level up their herbalism skill as well.

Too bad that they won't be able to come outside the city walls for quite a few more years. They would enjoy wandering through these woods, probably more than they will like visiting the city.

And do I even want them to transport to Neutram? What if they run into Nemesis? What if he tries to "test" them too?

I have to protect them both, but I don't know what to tell them about the situation. Neither one knows the truth about our status in the Realms. That I scammed our way into the game. That our player status is a lie that can be taken away.

At this point Nemesis holds all of the cards. I have to think of a way to get around that. To figure out his plan before he does more than send threatening letters or test my responses. Before he drags the rest of my family into his twisted plot.

I have to figure out a way to end his game.

# Chapter Twenty-Five

L G.'s green alarm clock breaks the early morning stillness. He carefully shuts it off and winds the clockwork with a large bronze key.

"I wish we didn't have to get up so early," Alby says with a big, stretching yawn.

"Too early," L.G. agrees. His yawn highlights his razor-sharp teeth.

"No more yawning," I say, but it's too late and I join them. "You two didn't have to get up. But I'm glad you did. It's fun eating breakfast together."

"And you want one of us to cook."

"Of course. Anything I can do to help you advance your training."

"Hah!"

"And one of you can make me lunch too." I smile.

"She just doesn't want to eat lumpy bread and burnt water," Alby says to L.G.

"Nah, lumpy water and burnt bread," he snickers.

"The sacrifices I make," I say with a dramatic tone as I raise the back of my hand to my left eyebrow. "Forcing myself to eat your perfectly prepared, absolutely delicious meals. Such hardship. But I do it all for your education."

This earns me a swat with Alby's pillow and a chuckle from L.G.

"L.G. and I drew up plans for the garden yesterday after class." She hands me a rather crinkled sketch.

"Nice. We can work on this over the weekend. I will have more seeds gathered by then."

"Sweet."

"Come on. I'll brush and braid your hair for you."

I sit behind my sister on the bed and pull the comb through her hair, working patiently through the tangles. I gather the long, silky hair at the top of her head, and let the rest hang down unbound. My fingers fly through the braid work. I tie a thin green ribbon at the end, double-knotting it so that it won't work loose.

"There you go. Very pretty."

Alby wrinkles her nose. "I don't want to look pretty."

"No?" I smooth the top of her head with my hand.

"I want to look otherworldly and vaguely threatening."

"I see." I scoot around so that I'm sitting in front of her. "Any reason why?"

She shrugs. "A lot of the kids at the school try to talk to me, but I don't want to talk to them. They ask questions I don't want to answer or treat L.G. like he's a pet or something. Someone who doesn't matter."

"Yeah," L.G. agrees in a quiet voice.

"When he's working at the alchemy table or something they try to push him out of the way. And they're surprised when they can't."

I nod in understanding. L.G.'s special status means that he can't be treated like an NPC. He can't be pushed around by the other Players.

"Sounds like you two are frustrating them."

"You think so?" Alby perks up a little.

"It's important to learn how to deal with people like that. Who are mean, obnoxious, or idiots."

"What did you do, when you used to go to school? When kids were mean?"

A half-smile creeps across my face. "Once. I didn't react well. There was kicking involved."

"Did you get in trouble?"

"No. The other kid was several years older than me. Twice as big really. The teachers thought I was a victim. But I wasn't, which is why he never bothered me again."

"Can't kick at school," L.G. says. "No PVP allowed."

"And that's a good thing." I reach down and rub behind his horns. "My advice is to figure out what these bullies want, and then don't give it to them."

"Yeah?"

"Frustrates them to no end."

"Yeah!" L.G. smiles.

"They can't hurt you. They can't even touch you. And their words mean nothing unless you give them meaning."

"Okay." Alby reaches over and gives me a hug. "Come on L.G. Let's get cooking."

Their enthusiasm is infectious. I hurry through my own morning routine, brushing and braiding my hair so that it stays close to my head. I don't know what the morning holds, and if I fight in fae form, my opponent will not be able to grab a handful of hair.

I've been remiss in training. I haven't practiced with my new spells. True I can sort of figure it out with math, but that's not the way my brain functions. Practice, observation, repetition. Figuring out each type of fight with different variables. Seeing what does the most damage. Which combinations work best.

**Fae Fire** seems to do the same amount of damage as **Claw**. The only benefit I can see is that **Fae Fire** is a ranged spell, while I have to be up close and personal to attack with **Claw**. Oh, and it uses mana instead of energy. That's important.

I'm still not certain what benefit **Nightfall** will be, or why I would want to basically cause a 50 yard blackout, but I'm sure I will learn.

Enough of this. No use worrying.

"Wow. You two have been busy," I say as I walk into the kitchen. "You didn't cook this all in the last few minutes, did you?"

The makeshift table we constructed last night from a large board balanced on four logs is covered with plates of buttered toast and cups of hot chocolate. Two dishes of breaded eggplant chips smothered in salsa steam invitingly next to a large chef's salad. A bowl of oranges and apples sits in the center of the table.

"We cooked this yesterday. The eggplant is still hot!" Alby's enthusiasm shows.

"The magic bags are amazing." I pick up a dish of eggplant and scoop up some of the salsa. "Is that mayonnaise?" I ask after taking a bite.

"Yep. I learned to make it." L.G. flashes his toothy grin. "It has olive oil, mustard, salt, and eggs-plant in it."

"Eggs-plant?"

"It's a special plant that grows eggs."

"Of course it is." I shake my head. "Sort of an egg-substitute I'm guessing. I haven't encountered those in the realms yet."

"L.G. And I have been watching the Auction House for seeds. We've got a few eggplant and eggs-plant."

"You use a lot of eggs-plant in cooking," L.G. explains. "You can buy them from a vendor, but it's cheaper to grow your own."

"Well, I have a surprise for you two. I reached the next level of Herbalism. Whenever I pick something, I have a 100 percent chance of getting both the item and a seed."

"Cool!" They chorus.

"When we do plant some of those higher-level flowers, herbs, and plants in the garden, you two should take turns harvesting them. You can level your own Herbalism that way."

"I can't wait for the weekend." Alby nibbles at her toast.

"Me too." L.G. agrees. "We can work on the garden."

"Can we visit Neutram too? I'd like to look around," Alby asks with a pleading look in her eyes.

"If we have time. I'd like to get the garden in first. I'm not sure how long that will take." And, of course, I have to figure out what to do about Nemesis. But I don't say that out loud. No use worrying them. "There's plenty of time. We don't have to rush."

"We have a surprise for you," L.G. says, then casually takes a sip of hot chocolate.

"Really?" I look at my sister. Her lips are pressed into a thin line, which means she's suppressing a grin. "What have you two been up to?"

"We've earned gold." Her eyes sparkle. "We've added almost a thousand to our bank."

I stop in mid-bite. "How?"

"We sold a lot of the potions we made on the Auction House."

"Low-level flowers and herbs too," L.G. adds. "Those are in high-demand."

"Players don't want to go out and pick them for themselves."

"Lazy."

"Yeah."

"I …" My voice breaks and I clear my throat. "I'm so proud of you two."

"Hey, you always say, all for one, one for all. Right?" My sister smiles.

"We're in this together."

"Right." I pause for a moment. "You two will have to fill me in this weekend when we work on the garden. I want to know your secrets to success when selling on the Auction House."

"We have another surprise." Alby piles twenty sandwiches wrapped in wax paper on the table. "This is for you. So you don't get hungry on the airship."

"They have tomatoes. And mayonnaise. And green leafies." L.G. digs into his salad with gusto.

"They also have a 5 percent health and attack power buff. It lasts one hour."

"Thank you. I'm … going to be really full."

"Don't eat them all at once, silly. The buff doesn't stack."

"You guys take such good care of me." I blink back the moisture in my eyes.

"It's a sacrifice for sure."

"Yep. Such hard work," L.G. agrees. "But you're worth it."

# Chapter Twenty-Six

I port to the city and follow the quest GPS line until the airships come into view. Two are currently moored to a platform on top of a large stone tower.

There's a guard at the base of the tower and he checks my name on a list before he lets me climb the stairs. He's a regular Neutram City Guard, and he seems competent and alert.

"The Stormherald is docked on the east side," he says, waving me along. I nod, though I plan to follow the GPS line to my destination.

The sun hasn't peeked above the horizon yet, and there is a touch of coolness in the air. A breath of late fall. I don't know if they observe it in the Realms, but I smile thinking about celebrating Thanksgiving in our new home. I certainly have a lot to be thankful for.

I'll have to try and find some pumpkins to gather. Pie has always been my favorite part of the meal. Alby's too, although she prefers apple or cherry. We already have so many of those fruits stored in the bank, we don't need more. I wonder what L.G.'s favorite will be. Probably something green. Maybe Key Lime pie? I'll have to look for limes as well. I never saw any tropical fruits in the Starter Zone. Maybe Myke will know where some trees grow. I hope my two little chefs can learn the recipes, but even if they don't I will give it a try.

The pies will end up lumpy and burnt if I bake them. I know it. But it's the thought that counts. At least that's what I tell myself.

"That's a nice smile." Sertaiven stands near the walkway that links the Stormherald to the dock. "Happy to see me?"

"I was thinking about baking pies." I hesitate for a moment and then add, "and I'm happy to see you."

"I knew my charm would wear you down." He winks. "And you're right on time. I like a woman who's punctual."

"You know a lot of women that aren't punctual?" I ask, arching an eyebrow.

"Well ..." he tips his head to the side and grins crookedly.

"So are you here to see me off, or are you coming along on this trip?"

"You're looking at the official Ambassador of Neutram, thank you very much. For this mission anyway. Normally I'm not allowed to leave the city. Have to be here to defend it if trouble strikes. But the Commander made a special exception." He offers me his arm. "Care to come aboard, Miss Camille?"

"Cami," I correct him, but take his arm. "No need to be formal, Ambassador." I'm having a hard time understanding his purpose. Is this courtesy, humor, or something else?

"Permission to come aboard, Captain," Sertaiven calls as we are about to step onto the deck.

"Granted." Captain Nyrie Balere's appearance is startling. I had expected a human woman, but the AI identifies her as a level 40 Gunakadeit, a species who live near the coast and specialize in seafaring.

Interesting that she would choose to captain a ship that will never be in any type of water unless it rains.

"Welcome aboard The Stormherald!" The captain has a gritty, rasping, voice. Not unpleasant, but distinctive. She sticks out a large hand with copper-colored talons. "I'm Captain Balere."

I release Sertaiven's arm and shake her hand without hesitation. "Glad to meet you. Please call me Cami."

"Our special advisor. Gotcha." She tips a wink at me. "Come on and meet the crew."

The crew, all level 40 human NPCs, are hard at work. Their faces lift up to look at me when the captain calls their attention. Ten women and men. Trained soldiers. Mostly middle aged. No expression on those faces. But cracked and weatherworn from spending time in the sun.

They all wear blue and red uniforms, sailor's caps with polished bills, and heavy goggles. Balere has four epaulets sewn at the shoulders of her coat and a much fancier hat than the crew.

"Is it all right if I give the crew a magical buff?" I ask the captain. "It's called **Symbol of the Fae** and improves the armor and stamina of myself and my allies by 1% per level. It will be a 21% buff at my level."

"Be my guest."

After I cast **Symbol of the Fae** and the crew feels its benefit, they treat me with a lot more warmth. A few grins and some heartfelt thanks are tossed my way.

"That's a handy ability to have," Sertaiven comments.

"Imagine what it will do when I've leveled all the way up."

"It's pretty impressive right now."

Even though the crew seems standard, the mixture of NPC levels confuses me. The Traveler's Zone NPCs are supposed to range from level 20 to 40. Members of the guard, like Sertaiven, can be level 100. Just like the Forrest Guardians in the Starter Zone, they serve as peacekeepers. They have to be able to control players of every level. I wonder if this is why he needed a special dispensation to go on the journey.

A tingle of anxiety leaps into my chest. Sure, the Commander is allowing Sertaiven on this quest, but so is the game. It fits in the rules, whatever they may be. I'm still trying to suss that out. Which means there is a reason that a level 100 NPC is allowed, or needed, on this journey.

Something's up. I just don't know what.

The sun slips over the horizon. While there's still a chill in the air, the sun provides a gentle warmth.

"Cast off."

"Aye, Captain." The First Mate, Daniel Smith, busied himself among the crew.

"Set course for the Polyperibitians's First Village, Smitty. Full speed ahead."

"Does it have a name? The village?" I ask Sertaiven.

"Sort of. The Polyperibitians don't name their villages. They use numbers. Although some have developed names due to landmarks. Other races call the First Village the Crossing Village or Crossings because a tributary of the Wild River runs through the middle. The water's shallow and the villagers have placed stepping stones to make the passage easier. The tributary provides pure, clean water for the village. They even have fish traps and weirs placed strategically downstream. Makes getting fresh fish for meals really easy."

"So the First Village is the original one they settled in after leaving their homeland?"

"Not exactly. There was another settlement before the First Village. It disappeared. But no one outside of the Polyperibitians knows what happened or why they abandoned it. You should ask one of the elders when we arrive. They might be more forthcoming to a Traveler than they have been to our merchants or sailors."

This sounds suspiciously like the set up for a quest that I should be able to get from someone in the First Village. I'll have to be on the lookout for it when we get there. That quest sounds more interesting than the typical "rescuing a kitty from a tree" adventure. I have to be on the lookout for it when we arrive.

If we get there. The purpose of this trip is to present a tempting target for the pirates. And they could attack at any time. We might not reach the First Village today.

Speaking of pirates … I stare off into the distance, searching the horizon for any sign of gliders. I don't bother looking down at the forest. The ground is over a hundred feet below. From what I saw during the first attack, the gliders would not be able to maneuver in the trees. They would need a clear place to launch and gain altitude. As a fae who can shape shift to **Flightform**, I understand the nature of wind and using rising thermals to gain altitude.

"First time flying?" Sertaiven asks.

"It's my first time on an airship, but not my first time flying."

"What do you mean?"

"Fae have magic. We can transform to different shapes."

He leans back against the rail, crossing his arms. "I've heard about that, but I've never seen it. Not too many fae visit Neutram."

Maybe it's foolish, but I want to impress him. I focus my energy and **Transform**. My skin stretches. I double over and almost fall onto all fours. Within moments I have assumed the form of an onyx-colored panther. I look up at him, grinning.

The look on his face is almost comical. Then he reaches down and runs his hand through the fur behind my head.

I freeze at his touch, acutely aware of his hand caressing me. I hold myself rigid, unsure of what he is doing, or what I'm supposed to do.

"Amazing." He shakes his head and abruptly pulls his hand away, looking self-conscious. Like he overstepped his bounds.

I shift back to my regular fae form. I straighten, and he has to look up to meet my eyes.

"I … shouldn't have—"

"Would you like a sandwich?" I interrupt him. I don't know what else to say, but I don't want him to apologize. It would ruin the moment. "My sister and L.G. made me some tomato sandwiches."

"I could eat."

"They have a 5 percent health and attack power buff." I pass him a sandwich and take one of my own.

"It's good." He takes another bite. "They learned to make this at school?"

"Yep. Cooking is an essential self-defense skill for them."

"Self-defense?" He raises an eyebrow quizzically.

"They have to protect themselves from my cooking." I'm relieved to see him relax and chuckle.

"That bad, huh? I hear you. I've been known to burn water myself."

Now it's my turn to laugh. "I've been accused of serving lumpy water."

"That's … impressive."

We finish our meal in companionable silence. I hate to break it and linger over the last bite, but there is information I need to know.

"I've been thinking about why you are on this trip," I begin.

"The pleasure of your company is a big draw." He winks.

I'm not going to let him distract me with flirting. "You could have that back in the city. You just need to ask. You didn't have to risk life-and-limb."

"I'll remember that."

I lower my voice. "In part I think that you are here because of the leak you and your Lieutenant discussed in the café."

Sertaiven nods and smiles. This is not an expression that holds any warmth. It is as cold as sunlight on the snow. "I mean to bring back the pirates alive if I can. The Commander wants to interrogate them." He pats the **Zap Stick** on his belt. "Non-lethal force preferred."

"They'll be given a fair trial?"

"Yes. Within the laws of the city."

He only has the one **Zap Stick**, but he has at least half-a-dozen handcuffs attached to his belt. "Those are the cuffs you used in the city?"

"Yep. Since the suspects have magic, it's the best way to render them harmless."

"Can I have one?"

He unhooks a set and passes it to me. "I'll need that back by the end of the trip."

"Hopefully I can return it with a pirate attached." I slip the cuffs into my **Bag of Infinite Holding**.

A commotion on deck draws our attention. The airship slows, coming almost to a halt.

"What's happening?" I ask the First Mate as he scurries toward the pilot house.

"No worries, miss. We've sighted another ship is all. Parked outside of the shipping lanes. But they're flying under a merchant flag. Captain's ordered the semaphores. We'll see if they've any news or know of any pirate activity."

"They're not under sail and sitting too far away to launch an attack. No cannons can reach this far," Sertaiven says. "Those merchant ships are big and slow. Probably safe to contact them."

"But the gliders I saw attack the Woedboran's airship can cover that distance in moments." I bite my lip, thinking furiously. "They're fast."

"You think the ship's bait?" He scans the horizon. "There's no good place for the gliders to launch. They need a big field for a runway, or an elevated area. No cliffs or structures—"

I interrupt him. "Except the deck of that airship."

# Chapter Twenty-Seven

Sertaiven doesn't hesitate. He dashes to the upper deck where the Captain and her First Mate stand near the pilot house and calls out the potential attack. I'm fast on his heels and arrive just as Balere snaps a telescope to her eye.

"General quarters," she orders. "Run out the guns."

Smitty rings a large, brass bell three times. "Guns make ready!" The crew races to their positions, archers at the rail, and one man each at the fore and aft cannons.

There are clearly three gliders coming in. I wonder if that's all the pirates were able to salvage for this attack, or if they sent fewer gliders because of the smaller size of The Stormherald compared to the Woedboran's ship.

"Will they try to come aboard?" Sertaiven asks.

"They didn't in the other attack. But they weren't trying to capture that ship or its cargo. Just the Ambassador." I respond.

"Different situation then. Be prepared for an attempted boarding," he says to Balere.

"They won't get that far." The Captain stands calmly on the deck, her hands folded behind her, showing no emotion. "Gunners. Fire at will."

The pattern is pretty much the same as the attack on the Woedboran airship. Two of the gliders separate from the group and bear down on the front and the rear of the vessel. When they are barely in range, the cannon fires.

Instead of a cannon ball, or a scatter shot of stones, the cannon launches a weighted net. It wraps around the gliders, knocking them out of the sky. They drop like stones. Only the lines that attach the nets to the ship keep the pirates from plummeting to their deaths.

The timbers moan and flex in protest as the lines pull taunt with the added weight. The ship lurches forward and back, settling.

"Reel them in!" The Captain orders. "Prep the guns for the second round. Standard shot."

"Bring her around quick! Set course for the merchant ship. Full speed ahead," Smitty orders. He glances at Sertaiven. "No worries, Ambassador. We're twice as fast as the enemy vessel. They won't get away."

The crew hauls the pirates onboard and cuts the lines attached to the ship. The gliders free-fall and then hit the tops of the trees with a crash. The two men, both level 20 NPCs named Murry, are cuffed and kneeling on the deck. So I was right. Apparently, the crewmen all share the same name for some unknown reason.

If multiple Murrys are here, where is the Boatswain in charge of the mission?

Sertaiven frowns and looks around. "Where's the third glider?"

I lost track of it in the heat of battle. "Where is it … There!" I shout. "It's booking in the opposite direction."

"We can't go after both," Balere says. "The ship's the more important target."

I can't let that glider get away. "I'll get whoever's on there." They all stare at me, puzzled, until I shift with **FlightForm**.

"We've got to have a talk later about what exactly you can turn into," Sertaiven says. "You know, someday when we're not fighting for our lives."

I grin and spread my wings.

"Cami. Wait!" He throws a flare. I catch it in my claws and tuck it into my **Bag of Infinite Holding**.

"Set that off when you catch the pirate so we can find you in all that greenery."

I nod and fly off. I'm faster than the glider, so I catch up with it quickly enough. And I spot the pilot.

*Cheville Jambe*
*Boatswain of The Deadlights*
*Alignment: Hated*
*Level 30*

Although the AI supplies the information, I knew that somehow Cheville would be behind this attack. If she's here, where is Murry Two? Back on the pirate ship? Or did she stick a knife in his back like Murry One?

Enough of this speculation. I have to figure out how to bring the glider down without killing

Cheville or dying in the process. I can't use any of my cat-style attacks while I'm in bird form. I can't cast **Fae Fire** either. But because she's hanging from a glider, Cheville can fling fire-bolts at me which will do a lot of damage. Unless I keep moving erratically to dodge the bolts, or fly directly above her, she will eventually kill me.

Because of the glider mechanism, she doesn't have line of sight on me when I'm overhead. But I can see her around the edges enough to target a ranged attack. Not that this does me any good.

Except … an idea pops into my head. My shift to **Flightform** and to regular fae form is instantaneous. **Flightform** has a 60 second cool down. It takes one second to cast **Fae Fire**. It might be possible …

Even if this works I will look ridiculous. The sailors on both ships will get quite a show. But that doesn't matter. There are other things that matter more, and always will.

I soar higher, maintaining my position above the glider. The air becomes thin and sharp in my throat. I shift to fae form. My body plummets for 60 seconds as I wait for my cooldown. I target Cheville as soon as I come into range and cast **Fae Fire,** and then shift back to **Flightform**.

I beat my wings frantically to halt the free-fall. The glider wobbles as the damage ticks away. Cheville swears a blue-streak.

"Snogger! You'll rue the day yer mother ever spawned ye!"

But she can't get a shot off. And I can. Over and over.

I keep careful watch of my mana and energy. And careful watch of the flickering light that indicates the pirate's health. It shoots up a few times, indicating that she's taken a health potion, but the glider soon spirals toward the treetops, crashing down. The metal clink of her harness releasing is quickly followed by the sound of her feet hitting the ground.

I dart down, land behind a tree and shift into panther form. I cast **Shadowform** and creep forward. The spell renders me almost invisible but does not cover up the rustle of the leaves and needles on the forest floor.

Cheville plants her feet in the middle of a clearing, her hands illuminated by the gathered energy of her fire spell. Her eyes dart back and forth, looking for any sign of the enemy.

I weigh my options on successfully completing an attack. Not good. At level 30 she's 9 levels above me and has magical abilities that should not be available to an NPC. Who knows how strong her DPS really is? True, I have very strong gear thanks to the glitch in the Spider Queen's raid, but that may not be enough to protect me.

But a sneak attack could give me an advantage. I cast **Nightfall** on Cheville so even if she moves, the 50 yards of darkness will travel with her. The illumination, already dim in the shade of the trees, drops one level.

"Curse yer sorcery to the depths!" she snarls.

She can't see me, but I can see her. Those fire-sparked hands light up her immediate area, bathing her in a yellow and red glow. A thin wind springs up, rustling the branches of the trees and setting her flames whipping like burning pennants.

I creep up behind her, at the last moment invoking **Claw** and concentrating the strike at the back of her knee. As her leg buckles, her hands flail behind her back to break her fall. I

launch up and forward, shifting to my regular fae form and snap the handcuffs on Cheville's wrists before her butt unceremoniously hits the ground.

As my dad used to say, no matter how strong someone is, if you hit them in the back of the knee, they'll fall down.

# Chapter Twenty-Eight

"You didn't kill her," Sertaiven says. His voice is noncommittal, but I can tell he's deeply interested in my actions.

"I would have ended her life if I needed to protect my own. But I figured out another way. A better way."

"Better?" He nods toward the front of the ship where all the pirates, including those from the ship, are bound and, in Cheville's case, gagged to prevent a round-house cursing. "Once they stand trial before the Commander, I can't see anything for them except a date with the executioner."

"Better. Because it's not my decision who lives and who dies. If people start doing that, start treating life and death so casually, it all breaks down. That's just how life works. That's how people work."

Captain Balere wanders over. "We're ready to set sail for Neutram. Smitty is stationed aboard the pirate ship. He'll follow us to port."

"Evidence?" I ask.

"Bounty," she responds with a grin. "Bringing a prize ship back with us will be worth thousands of gold coins per head for the crew."

"You sure I can't convince you to sail back with us?" Sertaiven asks.

"I'm going to take the opportunity to explore. This is an area I've never been to, and I need to look for flowers, plants, and herbs."

"For your two little alchemists?"

"Yep."

"Well, be careful. And be sure to stop back at the Commander's office as soon as possible. He'll want to debrief you."

And so I can turn in my quest, I think. Aloud I say, "I have my **Residence Stone** with me, so I can get back home in the blink of an eye."

"Sounds wonderful. I'll have to get one of those someday." He clears his throat. "Before you take off, I was wondering if you have any plans for this weekend."

I hesitate. "I promised Alby and L.G. that we could work on a garden. And I hoped to show them around Neutram a bit."

"There's an open-air concert and fireworks on Saturday night in the park. If you're not busy, I'd like to invite the three of you for a picnic and to see the show." He rubs his hand on the back of his neck.

"I'd like that."

"It's not a date or anything," he assures me. "But I'll get the tickets for everyone."

I smile. "I'll bring the food. Made by Alby and L.G. So it will be edible."

I cast **Flightform** and drift down to the nearest clearing. When I land, I shift back to my regular fae form and watch until the two ships disappear over the horizon. Then I turn my attention to the local vegetation.

The late fall sun scatters gold on all sides of the grassy downs. Everywhere I look is rich with dandelions and long-stemmed marigolds. But these are common flowers. I cast my gaze wide, looking for the tell-tale glimmer of something special I can pick and bring home for my family.

"Hello, Freckles."

Where did he come from? How long has he been watching me? It's been a long time since I've felt this afraid in the deep, achingly deep, way that had been common during my life in the real world. After the Hydrologist took over my father's body, after his death, Alby and I were alone. And I was in charge. Our survival, more importantly her survival, depended upon me. Upon my decisions. There was no one else to turn to for help.

Society had broken down. People focused on themselves, on their own circumstances. Finding food. Finding clean water. Protecting themselves from accidental inscription by the human minds cast adrift in the water cycle.

There was no one who would take pity on two orphaned girls. No one who would help us. And Alby was too young to do much, although she tried. No—it was all up to me. And, even as I fought to keep us alive, that fear lurked inside and tormented my mind with a malevolent glee.

And now Michael appears. In the Realms. And because he helped me scam the system so that Alby and I could enter as Players rather than NPCs, his presence threatens my family. One word from him in the right ears could make our entire lives a living nightmare.

Is he Nemesis? And does it even matter?

"Hello, Michael." I'm on complete alert, every sense drawn sharp, feeling and listening for any quick movement on his part. For any indication that he didn't come here alone.

"You're looking good. Blue's your color."

"Thanks. You're looking … strange." Something's unusual. But what?

"That's a weird way to greet an old friend." He starts walking towards me.

"I wouldn't say we're friends." What is it? I stare at him, focusing all of my attention. What is it?

And then I know. "The AI isn't giving me a reading on you. It doesn't know you're in the world."

"What does it matter?" He throws his arms wide. "This isn't real. It's just a game. A diversion. You're trapped in here. You have no idea what's going on in the world."

"And you're here to enlighten me with a typical 'look upon your doom and despair' speech that every villain delivers at some point?"

"Villain?" He stops moving forward and stares directly into my eyes. "Is that what you think? That I'm the villain?"

# Chapter Twenty-Nine

"When you threaten someone, when you threaten their family, you don't come off as a hero," I say.

"Before this conversation goes any further along the path of uselessness, I will say two things. One—I've never threatened you or your family—"

"You didn't send me an in-game email a few months ago?"

"That's correct. I didn't send you an email."

"Wait …" He's playing word games.

"Sorry to disappoint you, Freckles. Why would I contact you? You couldn't help me. You didn't have anything I wanted."

"But I do now. Have something you want." I tap my **Bag of Infinite Holding**.

"The tablet will be useful to me. To our cause." He spreads his hands again. "It's of no use to you and I'm willing to pay a great deal to obtain it today."

I frown, ignoring his statements for the moment. "What's your second point?"

"I'm not the villain here. I'm trying to save people. Trying to save the world!"

"From who?"

"From whom."

I roll my eyes. "Is this really the time to correct my grammar?"

"I'm working with a group of people who have dedicated their lives to stopping the Hydrologists from inscribing the entire world." His face radiates angry concern. "Do you remember what we discussed in the hospital, Freckles? How the Aquariums breaking and the human minds leeching into the water system brought about a moment of clarity for the Hydrologists?"

#

*"I'm sure you know that some of the Aquariums became unstable—broke for lack of a better word—and the inscribed minds leaked into the world and were lost in the water cycle." He shakes his head. "Imagine being pulled from your own version of paradise into an unending void of confusion and pain, with no way to even cry out for solace."*

*His words make me sick, way down in the pit of my stomach, but my dad always taught me to face things head on without sugarcoating them. I might feel empathy for the inscribed people who are suffering out in the real world where they are lost, but their selfish desire to live in made-to-order paradises has fundamentally screwed up the world for the rest of us.*

*"Sounds like just desserts to me."*

*Michael ignores my comment. "Those problems are what got the hydrologists thinking. They were especially excited to learn that the inscribed minds could survive in the water cycle. Can you imagine? They had made these small, enclosed systems that eventually ruptured. Failure on an epic scale. What they need is an enclosed system that won't break." He smiles at me. "Guess what the ultimate enclosed system is, Freckles."*

*I shake my head. This is beyond me.*

*"You're sitting on it. The planet. Earth. The big blue ball. It's over 96% water, you know."*

*"This is…" I pause. "This is insane."*

*"I don't disagree, but there it is all the same. The new system couldn't be designed for just an individual, or a small family group,*

*like the Aquariums, so they're setting it up as
a worldwide MMORPG with a variety of inter-
connected realms.*

#

"You're trying to shut down the Realms?" I
try to keep my face neutral.

"No. It's too late for that. This place is
here. It exists. There are so many inscribed
minds in this place I don't think it could ever
be cleansed, although that would be ideal.
Restore the balance."

Killed. Not cleansed. He's playing a word
game again. But he's talking about killing
everyone in the Realms.

"So, what about it, Freckles? For old time's
sake? Sell me the tablet. You can name your
price."

"No."

"Really?" He tips his head and his eyes
gleam. "Not for any price? Surely there must
be something you want? Something you
need?"

"I'm not going to help you commit mass
murder!" I stop for a moment. Take a deep
breath. Continue on in a calmer tone. "You
offer money. What good will money be to me if

Alby and I are dead? If L.G. and everyone we know in the Realms is dead?"

"I could offer you something else," he says. His voice low. Soothing. "A way out of the Realms for you and your sister. Back to the real world."

"The re-inscription they were talking about in the hospital. Is that what you're offering me?"

He nods. "Yes. Although the doctors of A Single Drop are a bit behind my group in the technology. We've refined the process. A ninety-nine percent success rate."

"So you can put us back in our bodies?"

"Yes."

"Really? Our bodies? The ones that were drained and left as so much waste material at the hospital!"

"There's no need to get upset. I was speaking metaphorically. You would be placed in new bodies of course. Ones resembling your own."

"So I'll be a …" I struggle to think of a word. "A body thief. Put back into the dystopian mockery that was my life before I joined the Realms. And the prior owners of those bodies?"

"Are here in the Realms. Happy, so far as I know. Living the good life as players."

"I don't believe you."

"I'm not lying to you, Freckles."

No, I think. No, you're not. You may not be telling me the entire truth, but you're not lying about the bodies. About being re-inscribed. That's your get-out-of-jail-free card. "If you don't want to destroy the Realms, why did you attack MidWorld? Why plant the bombs?"

"To stop their expansion! When the Realms increase, our world decreases. If the Hydrologists of A Single Drop have their way, in a few years life on the planet will cease to exist. The only world will be the virtual one. We want to stop them. To contain their damage here."

"And you're going to let the Realms remain. Safe and sound? You're not going to try and eliminate the inscribed water completely? I don't believe you." My anger rises. "What happens to the people inscribed here?"

"We'll try to save as many as we can, but there are only a few bodies available for re-inscription. I think you said it best back at the hospital. 'It sounds like just desserts.'"

"You're forgetting something."

Michael tilts his head. "What's that?"

"All the NPCs that will be killed."

Michael stares at me. "You can't be serious. They're not alive. They're game-pieces generated by the Hydrologists. Part of the program."

"Simply beings inscribed on water molecules?"

"Yes!"

"Then what are Players? It sounds pretty much like what happened when I entered the Realms."

He waves a hand. "That's different."

"Why? Why is it different? How are their lives any less valid than our own?"

"NPCs in the Realms are created to serve human needs. Human interests. Their responses are dictated by an elaborate AI program. Are they intelligent? Yes. Are they self-aware? They have to be to make their reactions seem realistic. But are they conscious? Hardly. Don't kid yourself. Their programs could be over-written just like that." He snaps his fingers.

"You're saying they're disposable? That they have no free-will?" I shake my head. "You're wrong."

"Look …" he starts, trying to extend the argument. Trying to come up with an argument that I will believe. But I've had enough. I shift using **Flightform** and fly away before I physically attack him. Violence won't solve anything, although smashing his face would feel satisfying.

I don't want to deal with him anymore. I don't want to deal with his nonsense. NPCs are not disposable people. I'm not going to hand over the tablet and help him destroy the Realms. I won't be the one to sentence my friends to death alongside all of the Players in the game.

"Just think about it Freckles," he yells. "I'll be in touch."

There has to be a way to stop Michael from destroying the Realms.

I will find a way to stop him.

# Chapter Thirty

"So that's the story." I grip the arms of my chair, studying Tanyl's face for clues. Since I arrived at his home, he has been silent for the most part, interrupting my narrative only to ask for an occasional clarification. I've told him everything about Michael except the part where Alby and I scammed our way into the Game. I don't know how he would react to that information.

He leans back in his chair, steepling his fingers. "Do you believe this man? That he will attempt to destroy the world? That he has the means to do so?"

I nod. "If he has help on the outside, there are tools he can use. Chlorine, maybe other chemicals, can clean water of its inscription. If they're organized, they might have bombs. Rockets. Other delivery systems. They could target Challenger's Deep and destroy it."

"But your former world is in ruins. Is it likely that Michael and his friends have this type of technology?" He stares into my eyes—right into my head, it seems—and I find it impossible to look away.

"I don't know."

He takes a sip of tea. "Why did you choose to tell me? What is it you think I can do?"

I shake my head, frustrated. "I hope that you might have a few ideas. You know a lot more about this world than I do." I pause, afraid to let too much emotion show. "As to why I told you. I trust you. I don't believe that garbage about NPCs not being people. I don't see any difference between you and me, despite all of Michael's arguments to the contrary."

"Interesting," Tanyl says. "I will consider the situation. We will talk again very soon." He pauses. "May I consult with Myke and bring her up to speed?"

"Yes, of course."

*Congratulations! You have impressed your trainer. Amity with Tanyl Xillamin increased by 1000.*

*Alignment: Exalted.*

Well, this is intriguing. But before I can focus on the implications of my new status, the AI chimes back in with more information.

Quest Complete! **World II: The Game**.
Reward: **Portal Orb**
Level: Legendary
Designation: Unique

Congratulations player! By completing the quest **World II: The Game** at maximum difficulty, you have earned a **Portal Orb.**

**Portal Orbs** allow travel between distant points in the Realms. Unlike **Transport Portals** that link between two specific points or **Residence Stones** that transport the user to a specific area, a **Portal Orb** can transport a Player and his/her group to any point in the Realms regardless if there is a Portal placed at the destination. In addition, the user need not have ever visited in order to teleport to an area.

This item is designated as Unique.

I turn the Portal Orb over in my hand. The surface is smooth and polished a dark ebony color. Like the slick eye of an undersea monster with three holes spaced evenly on the surface.

Really, the orb reminds me of a bowling ball. I wonder what will happen if I stick my fingers in the holes?

"There's only one of these in the entire Game?"

Tanyl nods. "That is generally what unique means." He waves his hand at me.

*Quest Offered:* **World III: The Game.** *Difficulty May Vary. Reward: Unknown. Yes or No?*

"Yes." I say.

The clock on Tanyl's mantel chimes three times.

"Oh, I have to go. The school gets out at 3:30 and I need to grab something for dinner." I push off from my chair. "I don't want Alby and L.G. to cook every night. They need some time to relax."

"Before you dash off, I would like to remind you of something," Tanyl says, walking me to the door. "You have an important source of information in your possession. Perhaps it is time to use it."

I frown for a moment. "The tablet?" I sigh. "Why didn't I think of that?"

But I know why. It isn't my property. It belongs to Darlene. I didn't take it out again because using someone else's item seems wrong.

I've got to get over this. I didn't hesitate to scavenge before I was inscribed. When Alby and I were struggling to survive after dad died. Is this any different?

"I'll look into it tonight and tell you what I find."

"Good." He smiles, an expression which I always find a bit surprising. It seems so alien on his face. "Learn something. Improve your mind."

I walk to town and place an order with Nellie for dinner. Some of L.G. and Alby's favorites. She's waiting on other customers and doesn't have time to chat, so I take the opportunity to walk around and stretch my legs.

Old Town seems much smaller than I remember. Has it only been a few days? I smile. After my adventures in Neutram, Old Town seems quieter. Peaceful. And the hazy sunlight and the warm air make me feel sleepy.

A wagon pulled by two sturdy, shaggy horses crosses my path. The farmer, an older human male NPC named McDonald, is bringing a load of corn to the mill. I've completed a few quests for him and wave as he drives by. He tips his hat with a smile and draws up near the water trough. The horses lower their muzzles and drink.

Another NPC, the miller, rides by, his mount stepping high and shying at the shadows cast by the trees that line the street. The sunlight sends a dancing warm radiance through the fall-colored red-gold leaves.

I spot the glowing mailbox in front of The White Rose Inn and angle my steps in that direction.

*You have mail.*

Three letters. I'm popular it seems.

The first is a note from Commander Platt thanking me for my assistance and requesting my presence tomorrow morning for a debriefing.

With the second thank-you note, Captain Balere has sent an attachment. I open it to find 5 thousand gold, my share of the bounty from the sale of the pirates' ship. She also makes an offer for me to join her crew should I ever wish to earn more profit.

Wow. This gold will help. A lot. There are so many items Alby and L.G. need for their educations. I'm happy that I will be able to provide.

They're my family. Both of them.

The third letter has no return address. But it is signed.

*Having fun yet?*
*Nemesis*

###

# About the Author

Chris Pavesic lives in the Midwestern United States and loves Kona coffee and all types of speculative fiction. Between writing projects, Chris can most often be found reading, gaming, gardening, working on an endless list of DIY household projects, or hanging out with friends. She blogs on chrispavesic.com and Tweets @chrispavesic

# Dedication

For Dad and Breene, the best beta-
readers in the business.

# Acknowledgements

My deepest appreciation goes to my editor, Sloane Taylor, for helping me to clarify my vision.

A special thank you goes out to my brother, Jim, who surprised me years ago with a copy of World of Warcraft (vanilla) saying "this looks like some-thing you might enjoy." Thousands of game hours later, he had no idea what he was starting. Or maybe he did—I can never tell with my brother.

Thank you to my guildies, especially Larry (Mari) and Erik (Riaven) who have played almost every interesting MMORPG and Co-Op out there with me.

Thank you to all the members of Authors Moving Forward for your inspiration and help.

My heartfelt thanks go out to my family and friends for more things than I have room here to list.

I thank God for helping me achieve my dream and giving me the strength to strive for new ones.

Last, but not least, thanks to readers of this series. My book is only possible because of your enthusiasm and support. Simply put, you rule!

# Other books by this author

Please visit your favorite retailer to discover other books by Chris Pavesic:

**Starter Zone** *Book One of The Revelation Chronicles* Available in ebook, print, and Audible

When hydrologists inscribe the consciousness of a human mind onto a single drop of water, a Revelation sweeps the land. The wealthy race to upload their minds into self-contained virtual realities nicknamed Aquariums. In these containers people achieve every hope, dream, and desire. But governments wage war for control of the technology. Terrorist attacks cause massive destruction. The Aquariums fail. Inscribed human minds leech into the water cycle, wreaking havoc.

Street gangs rule the cities in the three years since the fall of civilization. Sixteen-year-old

Cami and her younger sister Alby struggle to survive. Every drop of untreated water puts their lives in peril. Caught and imprisoned by soldiers who plan to sell them into slavery, Cami will do anything to escape and rescue her sister. Even if it means leaving the real word for a life in the realms, a new game-like reality created by the hydrologists for the chosen few.

But life in the realms isn't as simple as it seems. Magic, combat, gear scores, quests, and dungeons are all puzzles to be solved as the sisters navigate their new surroundings. And they encounter more dangerous enemies than any they faced in the real world.
Time to play the game.

*Unquiet Dead* Book One of the *Chiaroscuro Chronicles* Available in ebook, print, and Audible

Chris Pavesic, author of *The Revelation Chronicles,* invites you to experience the first novel in the intriguing realm of Chiaroscuro. In a world of steam-powered technology and magic-wielding fae, mystery, intrigue, romance, and adventure fill a series sure to delight fantasy fans everywhere.

When the Temples north of Chiaroscuro are burned and followers of the Sun Goddess are murdered, Catherine, a bard of the Ealdoth Temple, sets out to find those responsible and to bring them to justice. With only the help of a traveling group of minstrels and a retired fae investigator, Catherine must solve the mystery before more people are killed.

So saddle up your clockwork mount, buckle on your electro-dagger, and join Catherine as she finds herself pitted against members of her own Temple, rogues members of the Seelie Court, and a seemingly unstoppable army of undead.

***Fierce: She Will Rise*** Available in ebook and print

In this wide-ranging collection of steampunk, dystopian, and fantasy short fiction, award-winning author Chris Pavesic presents vibrant female characters in compelling narratives.

This rich compendium includes previously published stories as well as new fiction.

Praise for "Going Home": "This is an excellent short story that is full of surprises for the reader. Martial law is about to be imposed in the colony. A secret room, trips on a train and a clandestine meeting are all part of this superb steampunk short story. Most highly recommended."--Off Grid & Loving It

Praise for "The World in Front of Me": "This reminded me a lot of the Lakeside community in Neil Gaiman's American Gods, but I won't say anymore about that for fear of giving away spoilers. But fans of Gaiman should really enjoy this story. Fans of strong women who make tough choices should enjoy this as well."--Karissa Sluss, Author.

Praise for "Heart & Mind": "The author has managed to weave an intricate web about being true to yourself. One shouldn't be guided or led by others. Above all, feel the magic in your own heart."--Chief, USN Ret...VT Town

www.ingramcontent.com/pod-product-compliance
Lightning Source LLC
Chambersburg PA
CBHW071446170626
46811CB00007B/2494